Best
Short
Stories

Book Two

By AZ Writers

Fogarty, Pat, ed. Best Short Stories Book Two by Az Writers.
Prescott. Granite Publishing October 2018 Print.

ISBN 978-1-7328121-7-8

Granite Publishing
Prescott & Dover

9 8 7 6 5 4 3 2
First Edition

Printed in the United States of America

Cover Design by Mariah Sinclair
Cover Photo by Jared Verdi

HBBXN 1551065906

Acknowledgments

Without the collective efforts of a fine group of writers, this compilation of *Best Short Stories Book Two* by AZ Writers would never have become a reality. I would like to thank each author who contributed to this project. A special thanks to Roger Antony, Dan Mazur, Sandy Nelson, Greg Picard, Bill Lynam, Mark Wenden, Bruce Paul & Dennis Royalty for their extra efforts to bring this multi-genre collection to fruition. This compilation of Short Stories is a result of the combined efforts of Joe DiBuduo, Toni Denis, John Maher, Steve Healey and myself—Pat Fogarty—the elected board members of The Professional Writers of Prescott. Jerry Lincoln also deserves thanks. Jerry unselfishly filled the gaps with her expert knowledge of publishing and distribution. And, a special thanks to my bride Susan for her organizational skills, common sense advice, and encouragement. Pat Fogarty: Editor

Reviews

New York Times Best Selling Author Mike Rothmiller writes . . .

"Best Short Stories Book Two by AZ Writers is an impressive collection of stories written by an eclectic group of Arizona writers. You'll laugh, you'll cry and more importantly, you'll enjoy the book. The wide-ranging subjects hold your interest and make the reader eager to continue. It's well worth your time."

Best Selling & Award-winning Author Sam Barone Writes . . .

"Not much is assured in life or literature, but here's one guarantee you can count on – in this collection of stories you will find several that will make you glad you bought the book. AZ Writers produced an impressive body of work. One story made me laugh aloud, another brought back nearly forgotten memories, and one touched my heart. So, your favorite stories, the ones that will reach out only to you, are waiting for your discovery."

Award-winning Author Diane Phelps Writes . . .

This collection of human-interest stories by AZ Writers runs the gamut from humorous to touching to unexpected endings (and some beginnings). Several Stories present poignant childhood memories we all can relate to. You'll also like the editor's choice of quotes from well-known authors. Overall, "Best Short Stories Book Two" makes for a well-written and engaging read. It's a very entertaining collection of Short Stories.

Diane Phelps is the author of The *Un-Common Raven*: one smart bird.

Preface

"Best Short Stories Book Two" by AZ Writers contains 34 captivating stories written by more than 20 different authors possessing an outstanding range of talent. Unlike many other Short Story collections, in this book, the reader will experience the writing voice and style of many authors. Whereas in most other collections the reader is confronted with a dozen or more stories written by one author who writes stories with the same voice, the same style, and usually with the same plot, which after a story or two, become quite boring. Or, as in some other collections, the reader will find stories written 100 years ago by authors who are no longer with us. In "Best Short Stories Book Two" the reader will find a contemporary multi-genre collection of stories by dozens of authors who are still, as of this writing, on the green side of the grass. This collection of Short Stories includes memoir stories, historical fiction, creative non-fiction, and many other well-written pieces that will amuse, intrigue and captivate the reader. A few of these stories may make you laugh, and a few may bring a tear to your eye. In this collection, you will find well-crafted stories with irony, sarcasm, adventure, mystery, crime, and a couple of stories with a bit of romance.

El Toreador
By Greg Picard

"YOU WANT IN ON THIS, BOSS?" Tom Seaton had a raised brow, with a questioning turn to his face. Mr. Spock, on the bridge of the Enterprise, would have been proud.

"Why not, I haven't had my daily dose of stupid yet." Ranger Chris Becker obviously wasn't happy at the moment. "I would just like for once to have an ordinary day with happy park visitors and nice weather. No drugs, no thieves, no cars crashed, and no lost persons…and all the upper management in Headquarters on vacation. Is that too much to ask?" He slapped his computer mouse down on the desk and scrunched his Stetson on his head and said, "Might as well look the freakin' part for this. Whose place did this come from?"

"Lots of the horsie set start out that way, but the only guy I know that's raising livestock down there is over in Rattlesnake Canyon. Jack Hammond."

"Bulls! For Pete's sake, it's like a damn Merrill Lynch commercial with the stupid thing running down the middle of Highway 79."

"Don't forget your red cape!" Seaton was at full smirk.

"Oh yeah, really funny! At least Dick Savage isn't in town. I don't even want to think what the park superintendent would do with this one. Do you think Earl Martin is around now?"

"His horse concession is shut down for the winter, but if he and his wife aren't visiting their daughter, I expect he's there taking care of the horses."

"Did you notify highway patrol?" Chris asked Tom.

"Yeah, they have a bullfighter on the way." Seaton taunted as they tromped down the stairs and through the receptionist's office.

"Jane, would you see if you can find a number for Jack Hammond and call and tell him we've got a bull that we think might be his running on the highway just north of Oakzanita. Then see if you can get Earl Martin. Fill him in and see if he'll meet us down there. Maybe we can get him to help us. He knows more about animals than anybody I know. The guy's trained bears and God knows what else, surely he'd know what to do with an adult bull," Becker said as they slammed the office screen door behind them.

As an afterthought, he pulled the door back open and shouted to Jane, "And call Frank from fish and Game and tell him to bring a grizzly-sized rifle ASAP."

When they got to the south boundary parking pullout, there was a crowd of cars parked. Though it was a light traffic day, a line of vehicles was starting to back up down the highway. People were trying to turn around, but some were just spellbound lookie-loos. Becker was spellbound as well. It wasn't a bull. They were looking at the nearly five-foot shoulder height of a 1,500-pound male buffalo that was alternating charging a now battered Chevy and a school bus and stomping the ground. The bison probably couldn't hurt anyone in the big bus, but the screams of the children were unnerving.

"Where's Clint Eastwood or Gil Favor when you need them," Becker mumbled as he whipped the patrol truck back out of range. People had begun to wave and holler at them to do something.

"I think I'd rather have Geronimo, boss."

"Bring the shotgun, Tom, and load it with all the slugs you can."

"I think that's gonna just make him mad." Seaton practically squeaked it out. The rage of the bull was even making him nervous.

"There is that possibility."

"'Course, he already looks kinda mad at that school bus. I don't blame him much. I never liked riding in one."

"I wish we could get all these people out of here somehow." Becker pulled out his belt radio and thumbed the transmit button. "Montane, C537"

"537 Montane," Jane answered from the office.

"Did CHP give us an ETA on their units?"

"They should be there by now from what they said. They had two units coming from Alpine."

Tom turned to Chris, "Maybe we could take the patrol truck and turn the siren and lights on and distract the thing…maybe herd it toward the East Mesa Road up toward Oakzanita trail. That's probably how it got here anyway."

Becker was reluctant to try to shoot this monster with all the people around, and somehow even though it was likely destined to be burger patties by the rancher, he just felt bad about killing it. The press would have a field day with it, and Park Superintendent Dick Savage would blame Chris.

"O.K. let's give it a try."

"I sure hope we can keep him from goring us. Savage will have a cow if we mess up the truck," Tom muttered.

"Cows? Let's not get any more livestock involved in this than we have to, OK," Becker laughed.

Seaton took over driving and brought the truck up close to the traffic jam and flipped on the lights and siren and kept hitting the horn. At first, the buffalo took no notice and was still hammering the bus, but as they moved to the front, he suddenly stopped and stiffened his forelegs and dipped his head as he moved to face them.

"Uh oh, I think he's figured out we're here," Seaton said as he flipped the wheel to circle around the bull.

Chris cradled the shotgun out the passenger window and said, "See if you can make him follow us toward the fire road. Besides, he'll do a lot less damage to our back bumper than the front or sides of this thing."

As they were weaving in circles and dodging the bison's charges they took several hits to the rear step bumper and bed. It would have been comical if it hadn't been so dangerous. It wasn't looking good, but at least they were moving the bull back toward the fire road entrance. As they struggled to tease with the snorting bull, Chris caught movement out of the corner of his eye. Charging at them full tilt was Earl Martin on the biggest white stallion Becker had ever seen. He wore thick chaps and was swinging a lariat over his head as his horse dove toward the rear of the buffalo. As he threw the rope the loop snagged one of the bison's rear legs and the horse pulled up short snapping the rope tight. The bull was surprised and positively annoyed. When it turned to face the rider, Tom took the opportunity to turn and charge the beast with the truck. Confused, the animal couldn't figure out who to attack and stood still snorting with its head down. Martin took advantage of the distraction and backed the horse to tension the rope. Finally, the animal made a decision and turned to charge Earl.

Chris raised the shotgun thinking he'd have to shoot the bull for sure, but it seemed Earl was prepared for this and dropped his rope turning his horse to the fire road entrance. The bull followed full speed.

"Go, he's got him on the fire road, let's box him in from behind and keep him moving."

"Damn, I hope Earl's faster than that bison, I don't think we're going to have to do much to keep him moving."

"Did you see the size of those horns on that thing?" Becker said as he kept the shotgun at the ready. Becker hadn't had much time to marvel at the power and majestic size of the bison or its horns, but he was wondering about the fate of the bison in America as they tried to remove this one. Millions had roamed the central third of the United States for millennia. They kept the plains soil tilled and fed and clothed long lost Indian civilizations. It seemed a shame to kill this example in a park dedicated to the preservation of nature...not to mention the bad PR it would engender and all the nagging he'd have to hear from Dick Savage.

Seaton glanced at the rearview mirror, "Take a look behind us boss, I think the rest of the posse just arrived."

Becker turned to see two fish and game Broncos bouncing and fishtailing in the dust cloud behind them. "Well, at least they'll have a rifle that can reliably drop this bull if we need to." Again, it bothered him to think of shooting the bison.

Seaton was fighting the wheel in the rutted road, "When is this animal gonna get tired of running! We'll be at the Oakzanita trail junction in a minute. I hope Earl sticks to the fire road, so we can follow. That trail won't get the bull back to Jack Hammond's place."

Becker sighed, "I can't believe I'm chasing a buffalo in a pickup truck on a Tuesday morning. Whoever heard of herding with a pickup anyway? OK, when we get near the trail split-off, you back this truck way off and let the bull focus on Earl. I just hope he knows where he's going and what he's doing."

The turning point was at an oblique angle, and Martin didn't even slow as he peeled off left to keep to the fire road.

"Either he wants maneuvering room, or he's got a plan and knows where he's going," Seaton hollered over the engine as he gunned it to close the distance back up behind the bull and keep it moving.

As they rounded the next bend, they were joined by another rider approaching from the opposite direction. When he saw Earl Martin and the bison, he kicked his horse forward at a canter and rounded on the bull. The animal faltered for a moment and then charged the new rider. The rider was purposeful and appeared to know what he was about. Chris guessed he wasn't a casual recreation rider and must have been one of the ranch hands or Jack Hammond himself.

"Do you recognize that guy?" Becker asked Tom.

"I met Hammond once, and it's not him, but I'm betting it's one of his hands."

Between the two riders milling back and forth and the park service truck noisily gunning and blaring its siren, the bison finally seemed confused about its mission. As Chris watched the tiring animal stall and paw the ground, the ranch hand slipped his rifle out of the scabbard and shouldered it in one fluid motion. Before Chris could blink, he had fired two shots.

The bison shuddered and stumbled. It took two steps and turned toward Chris. At that moment as the huge brown eyes looked at the two rangers, Chris felt a sense of sadness he couldn't quite explain. The buffalo was just doing what it was made to do, running free and mounting a defense under what it perceived as a threat, and chasing predators from a herd that had already vanished 150 years ago. It was sad that a magnificent animal like that and his male brethren were to now be only sperm donors for future hamburger patties at Safeway, and BBQ steaks at yuppie parties.

The hand stepped off his horse as the buffalo dropped to its knees and crashed onto its side on the ground. Its great hairy head blew two snorting breaths that raised puffs of road dust…and then nothing.

"Looks like you guys have been having an interesting day," the warden behind them said as he slammed the door to his vehicle and walked up to Chris and Tom. "Everything OK here?"

"Looks like. Thanks for coming, Frank," Becker said. He had forgotten all about the wardens following them.

"Shame you had to kill it," the other warden said as he walked up from his truck.

"Naw," the ranch hand said as he walked past the dead bison, "the owner, Mr. Hammond, was gonna give up on the bison meat business anyway. Not enough demand yet, and the bulls are just too hard to manage. Too much investment in fence. He's gonna go back to cows. Lots better dispositions."

"You got a plan for this one?" Chris asked.

"Yeah, I'll bring up the bucket loader, and we'll haul it out. Take me a bit to get it here though. You guys mind watching the carcass for a bit?"

"Yeah, we'll stick around," Chris said.

The wardens eventually took off, and Chris thanked Earl Martin for his help. He told Tom to take the truck, finish his camp check, and tend to the park. After they left, Chris waited in the stillness with the dead bison. He wondered what it felt like to see a prairie filled with these magnificent beasts as far as the eye could see, and what skill it must have taken to kill one for food and its hide with only primitive weapons like spears and bow and arrow. He'd read somewhere that they sometimes chased the herd and drove dozens of bison off of a cliff to their death below. In some ways, it was little different than the white settlers and hunters coming with their efficient big bore rifles. Where there was a demand, mankind sought to fulfill it. Perhaps the Indians would have eventually decimated the bison as well. Sustainability was a concept that even now was a hard sell in modern America.

He felt like hiking once the bull was hauled off, and he walked the trails the rest of the morning back to his office. He couldn't get the look in the bull's eyes out of his head.

Egyptian Nightmare
By S. Resler Nelson

HE WAS GONE. Just like that. Only moments ago, my friend, Alex, had been beside me, guiding me as we shopped in the souks of Old Cairo. He was leading me through crowds in streets too narrow for cars. We were talking and laughing, and then he disappeared.

At first, I thought little of it. Surely, he'd just been sidetracked and had taken a quick detour into a shop to look at something that intrigued him. Any minute he would resurface, and we would continue sightseeing. But he didn't return.

Ten minutes passed, and it felt like an hour. I hadn't moved, remembering my father's advice when I was a child. "If you get lost or we get separated, stay put. It's easier to find one person than two."

Looking down the street in both directions, I tried to peer into each alcove. I didn't see Alex or anything else that looked familiar. I hadn't a clue as to where I was. Why should I? I had just arrived in Egypt today, and I was relying on Alex, who knew Cairo well.

Suddenly, I realized that I was a blonde female and a curiosity among the throng of dark faces. Egyptians passed by me—women with black, kohl-lined eyes lowered, and men in cotton full-length galabeya robes, with bold, almost seductive stares. I started to feel uneasy.

The street was dim, even with a hot, noonday sun overhead. The walkway was shadowed by balconies and overhanging canopies. Skeins of fabric, cotton robes and carpets hung from shop awnings. The smells of spices and urine, fruit, and perfumes mixed in the stifling air. And always the crowd, pushing in two directions like two streams running counter, moving in a singular sea, making me slightly dizzy.

A Muslim call to prayer echoed from a minaret, *"Allah Akbar,"* followed by melodious chants that drifted across the city.

Still, I waited, glimpsing at everyone, yet no one, trying to be inconspicuous, yet knowing I was obviously out of place.

A young Egyptian boy about thirteen appeared before me.

"Are you English, madam?" he asked softly.

"Yes," I lied, not wanting to divulge I was American.

"You need a guide? I can show you for a small price. Many things to see and buy. I show you," he said and reached out his hand toward mine.

Instinctively, I withdrew.

"I'm waiting for my fri . . . husband. He is showing me around," I answered quickly.

He looked knowingly at my ringless hand.

"I will be over there if you need a guide," he said and pointed to a café down the street. I watched him as he walked away and sat down among the men who were sipping coffee, talking, and smoking from free-standing water pipes.

Thirty minutes passed, and it was now clear that something was terribly wrong. I began plotting what to do next. It would be best to take a taxi back to my hotel and wait for Alex to contact me. If he didn't, I could notify the authorities. It seemed useless to continue standing in the middle of the souk.

The boy appeared before me again.

"Is madam still lost?" he asked.

"Of course not. But my husband has been detained. I will need a taxi."

"Yes, madam. Taxi no problem," he smiled.

He was a handsome boy, tall, thin, and unkempt. His curly black hair was scruffy, and his striped galabeya was stained and unraveling around the hem. He wore no shoes and his feet were calloused and dirty from walking the streets. But his smile was bright, and his brown eyes shone.

"Follow me," he said confidently, and I did. We continued in the direction Alex and I had been walking. He turned off the busy street into a dark, narrow alley. My heart quickened a beat, but I was in no position to argue.

Two emaciated cats hissed and growled at one another in the recesses of a closed doorway. They stopped, watching us approach. The boy stomped his foot, and the black one yowled and rushed behind me, causing me to gasp.

"I don't like cats," he muttered. "They are bad luck."

To my relief, the dismal backstreet opened into a slightly wider one. But it soon tightened and curved into another deserted alleyway that looked as though it would dead-end. Arabic music drifted from inside a dark opening. I failed to see how this was leading us to a taxi, and a sudden panic overcame me.

"Are you sure you know your way," I asked faintly.

"Do you know yours, madam?" he answered, and his voice sounded deeper.

I glanced behind me, hoping to see someone on the street, but it was still bare. How could one street be so crowded and another devoid of life?

"Perhaps we should be going the other direction," I suggested gingerly, still looking away.

When I turned to the boy again, a man was facing me. He was older, much older. One eye had been blinded and only a pale, whitish orb stared from the socket. A large scar crossed from his cheekbone to the corner of his mouth, causing his lip to droop. A long dark-handled dagger flashed in his hand. I wanted to scream, but no sound would come. Fear was choking me. Something cold and wet touched my hand.

I screamed so loud that I startled myself awake and bolted upright in bed. My collie whined anxiously and nudged my hand with his cold, wet nose. I recoiled, a leftover reflex from my nightmare.

"Oh, Laddie," I smiled and hugged his soft, sable coat, happy to find myself only dreaming. He looked at me curiously, with head cocked, and bounded from the room. I could hear my mother singing off-key in the kitchen, clinking dishes and silverware.

"Are you awake, Liz?" she shouted.

"Yes, Mother."

"Well, you'd better start moving. I'm fixing you a good breakfast for your big adventure. Your flight leaves for Cairo today, you know."

≈≈≈

After twenty-one hours of flights, the jumbo jet landed at Cairo International Airport. Alex was waiting and ushered me through customs and the crowds until we were outside hailing a taxi. After my nightmare, I planned to stick to him like pitch on a pine tree.

He was tall, dark, and handsome. Sorry to use the cliché, but he was, and I wondered why I broke up with him—other than the fact that when he moved to Cairo for an American Embassy job, I wasn't carefree enough to go with him. Seeing him now for the first time since he'd left the States, I might have to rethink that decision.

It was midday and hot. Alex said, "I thought we'd drop by the Hilton. You can check in, and then I'll show you around."

That's what we did, plus have lunch at the hotel. Afternoon and we were back in a taxi, headed for Old Cairo and the famous Khan al-Khalili souk.

"You'll love the shopping and the people. Such an international mix," he said, but flashes of my eerie dream emerged.

Once there, I have to admit the marketplace was colorful, expansive, and unique—wall to wall tourists from many countries and walks of life mingling with the Egyptians. We explored the souvenir shops, seeing everything from spices and curios to artwork and clothes, amidst lively Arabic music. I never left Alex's side. He probably thought I was clingy, and he was right.

As we moved with the flow of people, two busloads of Japanese tourists swept through, and I was carried along with them. When I tried to stop, I felt like a rock protruding in the middle of a river, so I kept moving with the current. Finally, they thinned out enough that I could anchor myself.

It was then I realized that Alex was nowhere in sight. I told myself not to panic; we just got separated. Stay put and he'll reappear. He'd be looking for me, too. Any moment he'd resurface, and we would continue exploring. But he didn't. Long minutes passed, seeming like half an hour, and his tall frame failed to crest above the crowd.

An Egyptian boy emerged before me. He was a striking child, lean and ragged, maybe ten or eleven years old. His wavy black hair was disheveled and his soiled, white galabeya robe was tattered around the hem. He wore no shoes, exposing youthful feet that were soiled and toughened from walking the streets. But his smile was genuine, and his dark eyes sparkled.

"Is madam lost?" he asked.

"No. My fri . . . uh . . . husband has been detained, and I'm waiting for him."

He glanced at my ringless hand and grinned. *Did he believe me?* He must know many tourists leave their jewelry locked in hotel safes.

"You come to my grandfather's shop and wait," he suggested. "You sit until you see your friend come by."

His offer was inviting. The overhangs offered little shade, and I wasn't used to the heat. Besides, I felt conspicuous standing alone as others wandered by. I imagined they were from all over the world, but they were *with* someone or in a group.

"Follow me," the boy said confidently, and for some reason I did. We continued in the direction Alex and I had been walking, and I thought if we walked much farther without seeing him, I would refuse to go on. My dream kept haunting me.

At this point in my story, you're thinking *take out your cell phone and call Alex. Cut the drama.* But I forgot to mention, the year was 1990 and cell phones were relatively new. In fact, the first portable cell phone emerged on the market in the 1980s, and the cost was prohibitive. The world was so different then.

I was about to ask the boy his name when he stopped near a dark, narrow alley. My heart quickened a beat. Two cats, mangy and scrawny, hissed and scowled at one another in a darkened doorway. They stopped quarreling, wary of us. The boy stomped his foot, and the black one yowled and scurried behind me, causing me to jump aside.

"I don't like cats," he muttered. "They are bad luck."

My eyes stayed on the cats, and when I turned back to the boy, a man was facing me. He was old and so hunched over that his galabeya touched the ground in front of him. One eye was covered with a well-worn patch. A large, jagged scar crossed from his cheekbone to the corner of his mouth, causing his lip to gape slightly. I almost gasped at the similarities between the old man and the one in my dream.

The boy frowned, not amused by my rude stare.

"This is my grandfather, Gamil. And I am Assad. Here is our shop," the boy said, with a sweep of his arms, gesturing at a small alcove, crammed with touristy items—oriental rugs, t-shirts, glass bottles of perfume oils, handmade sandals, and much more.

Assad asked my name.

"Elizabeth," I said, still holding back.

"My name means lion," he said with pride. "What does your name mean?"

"I have no idea," I answered, and he gave me a quizzical look.

His grandfather turned away and went about showing his wares to a couple of Middle Easterners. The shop was marginal, and I figured the old man and Assad struggled to earn a meager living.

I sat long enough to rest and reassess the situation, and then I rose to leave. At once, the boy was at my side, looking up at me with those deep brown eyes, and saying, "For a dollah I will help you find your friend. I know my way, and you don't."

I'd abandoned my "husband" references, as the boy didn't seem to be buying it.

Rather than meander alone, I agreed. "Okay, but we must go back the way we came."

Assad swept a dark lock of hair from his forehead and smiled, "Yes, madam."

I offered him the dollar, and he quickly took it from my hand. Then he motioned with a nod of his head, "Come . . ."

Alex and I had taken several detours as we walked, and I wasn't sure where I was anymore. I glanced back at the grandfather's shop. The old man didn't seem to notice or care that Assad was leaving with me, and that made me wonder about their relationship.

"We find him, madam. Not to worry," the boy said and moved out with a self-assurance that both amazed and concerned me. *Was I being foolish to follow him?* How many times had he "guided" a stray tourist for a fee?

But I kept stride with Assad—until I lost him, too. He slithered through a bunch of young men and vanished. The men were Egyptian, and they seemed rough. Most were bearded and muscular, wearing modern European clothes, and arguing among themselves.

Again, I was alone and distraught. Only this time, I decided to take charge. Surely a police officer would pass by, or I'd encounter someone fluent in English—maybe even an American tour group.

I stood still, considering my options, when Assad reappeared, pushing through the group of men with Alex close behind him. The boy seemed quite proud of himself when he realized that the man he led was the one I'd been searching for.

Alex gave me a hug and said, "This young man saw me standing alone, looking through the crowds for someone. We connected, and here I am. Clever boy."

He smiled at Assad, and the young boy beamed. "Sorry I lost you, madam, but I found your friend."

"You certainly did, Assad," I said, hugging him, not even considering if that was orthodox.

Alex relaxed his shoulders. "Assad says he's been watching over you."

"That's true," I said, a rush of relief enveloping me.

Looking down at the boy, Alex said, "This is for you." He slipped Assad a twenty-dollar bill. It would go a long way in his daily struggles.

Assad grinned and turned to me. "I have something for you, madam."

He held a small replica of a lion in his outstretched palm. It was handcrafted in reddish clay, and the lion's mane had been etched into shaggy strands. The likeness was crude which made me cherish it all the more. I knew he'd made it.

A thank you seemed inadequate, but I said it anyway. "Thank you very much. I will keep it always."

He smiled one last time at us and skipped through a throng of people before he disappeared.

We have the clay lion to this day—a reminder of Egypt and Assad and kindness.

The Traveler
By Greg Picard and Wendy Picard Gorham

SHE REMAINED SEATED, silent and unmoving, as Chris Becker slowly edged the State Park green pickup into the worn pavement spur of campsite 107 and shoved the gear-shift into park. The crunch of his tires made her turn and look, gray strands of hair dangling across her eyes. Inevitably, on camp checks, someone didn't want to pay, and it never worked out well. Even though law enforcement was part of his job description as a Ranger, it wasn't why he had joined California State Parks. He loved nature and wanted to encourage others to love it too. This was especially easy to do in a place like Humboldt Redwoods with its 300-foot-tall trees, their fluted red columns of shaggy bark fading into the moist morning fog above. Making first contact with a camper over a money dispute, however, was never a good way to start the relationship.

"Good morning!" she said. At least it was a pleasant start to the encounter. Sometimes people became eerily silent when 'the Man' came by to collect the $10 fee. They would turn away or make an effort not to be in camp when staff might come by. This friendly opener was far more encouraging to Chris, yet he was perplexed, upon his cursory examination of the campsite, to realize that she was camping with the bare minimum: a beaten and dented aluminum coffee pot and one small well-worn cast iron skillet sat on the grate above the remains of a slowly smoldering fire. A tarp draped over the picnic table as a makeshift tent barely sheltered a tattered and patched military issue sleeping bag beneath it, and at the far end of the bag, a faded blue rucksack had apparently doubled as a pillow.

His feet sank into the moist duff and needles as he moved off the pavement. "Kind of cold this time of year for just sleeping on the ground with a bag. We get a lot of rain here in the redwoods, too. Don't you have a tent?"

"I don't need a tent. If the picnic table won't shelter me, I can always use your laundry room for the night." She leveled her eyes on his, not really bating him, but not really innocent either. "'Sides, I got plenty of garbage bags to put on if the rain comes down too hard…stay just as dry as can be." She grabbed her sack from under the table with a weather-reddened hand and shifted from her place on the ground. With much effort, she finally got her leg up and under her enough to rise and grab the edge of the picnic table. Hoisting herself up, Becker could see she was straining and her pale color was not a good sign.

"You okay, ma'am?" His medical training was nagging at him now, and he wondered if he should just abandon the issue of the fee and consider her a patient. Becker was at least supremely glad she hadn't sought refuge from the weather in the laundry. At this late point in the season only a handful of campers were in the park at any given moment, and truly most of them weren't up in the woods to do their wash. If she had gone in there and had some sort of medical problem, he might not have found her for hours. It wouldn't be the first time some homeless person sought shelter in the laundry. Sometimes he wondered if he should replace the 'Laundry' sign with one that said, 'Social Services'.

"I'm fine; nothing a good cup of coffee won't cure…that and maybe being 30 years younger." She took a few slow steps toward the dwindling fire. She appeared to be testing her legs. It reminded him of a newly born deer he had stumbled upon years ago. Its mother had been killed by hunters, poachers actually, and it was taking lonely and tentative steps into a bleak and unfeeling world.

Stepping a foot or two forward, into the spot she'd just vacated, he smelled the distinct odor of alcohol…and onions from where she had stood.

"You traveling far?" he asked as she hobbled stiffly back to the table and lowered herself onto the scarred and cracked bench seat. He made a mental note that it needed to be refinished before the weather got too wet; with close to 80 inches of rain a year, nothing dried out in winter. It also brought into stark relief the level of multi-tasking this job required. He was really struggling with which hat he should be wearing at the moment: medical responder, law enforcer, nature protector, or facilities maintenance.

"Traveled far all my life. But travel implies you have a place to be going and a place to be from…now I've got neither. So maybe wandered is a better word." She pulled out a well-worn tin coffee cup from the pack at her side, "You want some coffee? I got another cup for company."

"You're traveling alone and homeless?" The realization began to dawn on him that perhaps he was going to have to channel a skill set that wasn't really part of the job description according to the State of California, and yet was something he found use for out here in the back of beyond more often than one would expect. He was going to need to listen. He was going to need to care.

"Homeless is such a dirty word, son. I'm not homeless. The world is my home." She made a sort of expansive gesture with her hand that was simultaneously profound and yet also kind of comical, like some down and out game show hostess still trying to point out the potential prizes to be won. Only in this case, at this moment, perhaps the beauty of this place was somehow the prize.

Chris hated to bring it up, but he figured it was time. "You know there is a $10 fee to camp here? I didn't find a pay envelope for this site in the Iron Ranger pay deposit."

"Yes, I know." Something in the timbre of her voice changed almost imperceptibly and some of the folksy slang element seemed to dissipate…almost as though she had been play-acting, and yet not really. Maybe more like another version of herself was emerging from inside the rumpled woman before him. It was strange and subtle, and Chris wasn't sure. He thought that he might just be imagining it. But when she spoke again, there was a definite shift. "I've got a Ph.D, so I did learn how to read. Unfortunately, I am cash strapped until my disability check arrives next week."

This was not what he had expected her to say. She was novel, and Becker was curious and decided to stall. "What's your Ph.D. in?"

"Philosophy. Most useless degree in the world, but I loved it."

Becker stifled the urge to chuckle. He knew it was misplaced and inappropriate, but he couldn't help but think of a few philosophy majors that he had known in college. The image he held of them in his mind seemed to support the possibility that they could have all ended up homeless…it seemed like a cerebral pursuit with little actual boots on the ground application. He was practical and pragmatic—perhaps to a fault sometimes—and he was skeptical of some of the things people chose to study in the hope of making a career out of them.

"Really? Wow…what did you do with it?" He assumed she hadn't graduated from a doctoral program and then immediately become homeless, and so suddenly he was keenly interested in connecting the dots.

"The only thing you can do with a degree like that…teach other poor unsuspecting students the useless art." She chuckled wryly and took a sip of the steaming black coffee. "Ah, nothing like a good cup of Joe." The colloquial vernacular seeped back in at unexpected moments, punctuating the juxtaposition of her circumstance. "I was at Duke for fifteen years. I loved that place. I loved that job. Thought I'd die still lecturing in those venerable halls."

"What happened?"

"Life happened, son—it always does."

They were both silent for a moment in the crisp autumnal air, as each digested that little bit of bitter truth. For Chris' part, his mind wandered to Lori and the baby. The last two years since Allie's birth had been a whirlwind, but not so much that he hadn't clearly felt the disconnect between himself and his wife. He wondered if that was just a natural part of life. Did children bring some couples together and somehow cast the distance of others into high relief? He couldn't shake the feeling that he was standing on a cliff with a tidal wave rushing down on him. It made him wonder if she had family out there somewhere.

"Ever get married? Any kids?" he asked.

The pause was so long Becker began to wonder if she was going to answer. "You never believe it until it happens to you." Her words had a faraway quality to them like she was talking to herself more than to him. He somehow knew he shouldn't interrupt, not even to encourage her, so he waited.

"She had been a beautiful baby, my girl Charlotte. She grew into a fine young woman. She was the kind who would take in every stray cat she saw; stray humans, too. She actually started a non-profit for orphans when she was sixteen. I think she was always looking for the father she never had in every man she knew. Unmarried, I had considered an abortion. I can't even wrap my mind around how empty life would have been without having known her. When she married that man, I cried like any mother would— watching her baby girl in white with a cluster of roses and a face full of hope. Not a year passed before I was crying again—only this time the bouquet was for her grave."

Chris sat in silence, transported through the raw power of her grief. He imagined attending his own daughter's funeral, and he couldn't even complete the thought without his chest tightening and his heart racing. He wanted to ask what had happened, but he couldn't make the words come. She must have read the question in his eyes.

"He wasn't a good man." She didn't say more, and he didn't pry, and yet a million scenarios played in his head while he waited for her to continue. "Foucault and Derrida couldn't explain how a man could strangle a woman with his bare hands and not be sorry. Suddenly I didn't have much use for philosophers. I didn't have much use for anyone."

They sat a few minutes more, letting the morning sun penetrate the foggy wooded coolness and warm them from the outside as the coffee did its magic on the inside. She stirred and began packing up her things.

"Can I give you a ride somewhere? I was thinking of getting a burger down in Garberville if you are headed south. There is room in the truck if you are thinking of going that way."

"A burger, at 8:00 in the morning?" She looked at him quizzically and Chris looked at his boots trying to hide from her gaze. Perhaps he should have instead been trying to figure out how to explain transporting a civilian in his Park truck without proper permission, but at the moment that didn't seem to matter.

"Ok, Garberville sounds as good as anywhere." She smiled and extended out the weather-reddened hand. "The name's Mae Redfield."

"Nice to meet you." He reached out and solidly gripped the woman's hand and then hesitated for a beat, considering how to address this ragged study in contradictions, then decided there was really only one choice, "Dr. Redfield. I'm Chris."

The ride through the southern half of the park's 55,000-acre ownership always gave Becker a lift. Massive coast redwoods lined the highway as it paralleled the river. Today it was within its banks. This winter, if the predictions were right, it likely would flood, perhaps leaving this same highway a dozen feet under water in places.

"So, you mentioned you are on disability, what happened?"

"During the murder trial," there was a pause and she breathed deeply, "I tried to kill the guy." She was so mattered of fact in her tone that Chris coughed and shifted uncomfortably. "The bailiffs who tackled me broke my pelvis in six places. I'm lucky I'm alive and can still walk at all. The head injury from being knocked around left me with epileptic attacks."

Chris was left speechless but managed a weak, "So where are you headed. Any place special?" He felt tension rising in the pit of his stomach and he was hoping to change the subject.

"Folsom Prison."

"Whoa," he reflexively took his foot off the gas for a second, then, slowly depressed the pedal again, "that sounds pretty serious." He knew some of California's worst felons were housed there.

"Yeah, it is serious. I have to meet someone. And it has to be Wednesday."

The small hairs on his neck rose up, "You have a meeting with someone at the prison?"

"Yes, we have unfinished business."

≈≈≈≈≈≈

The sun was shining brightly in Folsom as she waited along the front walkway. She sat on a bench with the .38 concealed under her backpack, just another homeless person loitering and looking for a handout. She watched as the door opened and thought *what goes around comes around* and fingered the trigger in her lap. Her eyes were fixed, unwavering, on the discharge door. She waited. There was a calm about her that belied the churning of her thoughts. She imagined lifting the gun slowly, taking aim, and feeling the cool metal of the trigger smooth against her finger. She imagined the glint of the sun on the barrel and the glint of fear in his eye the instant before the bullet found a home in his heart. She imagined....

From the corner of her eye, she caught movement. An attendant was pushing a man in a wheelchair out the side door. Visiting hours were over, so she wondered what this person was doing here this late in the afternoon. She was annoyed at the momentary break in focus this distraction had caused. She was determined not to miss her chance. But as the two approached, she could see the one pushing was a prison employee...and the realization dawned on her that the man in the chair was her daughter's killer.

Only fifty-three years old, but fifteen years of prison had taken a toll she had not expected. He was slumped and drooled from the corner of his mouth. Stroke. The vacant look in his eyes bespoke the lack of stimulation he could receive. It was as if the world around him didn't exist, and some inner dialogue was all he had. Perhaps he was out of one prison, but it seemed he would forever remain in another. She slowly watched as the attendant struggled and shoved to get him in the city's disability transit van.

She watched the van pull away from the curb and head out the long drive toward the main road, then put the revolver back into her pack, took a deep breath and slowly rose and walked toward the Folsom Lake campground.

"What goes around, comes around," she whispered, "one way or the other." *A philosophy of sorts*, she thought to herself.

Details make stories human, and the more human a story can be, the better.
—Ernest Hemingway

One Bronx Saturday
By Pat Fogarty

I WAS ELEVEN WHEN 'West Side Story' hit the silver screen. I did not know it, but I was growing up smack in the middle of a melting pot. In the early 1960's my South Bronx neighborhood consisted mostly of Irish and Italian Catholics, but we had a fair share of Finnish, German and Swedish Lutherans. They stuck together like a herd of moose. On the nicer neighborhood streets, a wealth of Jews lived in newer buildings and employed a smattering of Blacks as 'supers' and janitors.

So, when Ernesto Delgado moved into a nearby building, he was more of an oddity than a threat. Ernesto was the first live Puerto Rican I had ever seen. Living a block away in the Bronx meant he was in a different crowd than mine. We never called it a gang, because all we really did was hang out together and make sure kids from other crowds didn't pick on or bully one of us. On my street alone, there were a dozen small apartment buildings with about twenty kids in each one. With so many youngsters' running around, a firm rule voiced by our parents was to "Stay on the block, so I can see you." This edict was strictly enforced—the busybodies, yentas, and our mothers could look out a window and see exactly who was doing what. Some of the older women would place a pillow or cushion on their windowsill or fire escape and watch the street all day and into the night. If we stepped out of line, our mom might get a phone call and we'd be in for it.

Ernesto became friends with Jimmy Stanton, a kid I knew from school. They lived in the same building two blocks from me. Jimmy introduced me to Ernesto. And, even though they were in the 164th Street crowd and I was in the 162nd street crowd, we all became friends. We loved to play baseball and we were Yankee fans.

During the summer my parents would let me leave the block on Saturdays to play baseball on one of the fields near Yankee Stadium. There were six grass diamonds outside the famous ballpark and we always mustered up enough neighborhood players for a game. In the mornings before I left, mom would make cheese and mustard sandwiches, wrap them in wax paper and put them in a small brown paper bag. When I got thirsty, the public water fountain at the park was the best water in the world. With everyone using it, the water was always nice and cool.

On those summer days, we'd play ball from eight in the morning until late afternoon. Sometimes on a hot Saturday after a game, we'd head a few blocks over to the Harlem River where some of the guys would dive off an abandoned dock for a swim. I never went in. A few years earlier my mom had laid down the law about going in the river. As an eight-year-old, I had ventured to the river with some friends, collected blue crabs at low tide and brought them home. I got a beating and to this day, although more than a half-century has disappeared, I can still hear her words, "Young man, don't you ever go in that river again."

Well, that Saturday at the river we built a raft from pieces of scrap wood and broken pallets. It floated. Most of the guys jumped into the river and started to play "King of the Raft." Ernesto was holding onto a corner of the raft as the current started to drag it towards deeper waters. Jimmy was "King." I stood on the dock having as much fun watching, as they were having pushing each other on and off the raft. Ernesto managed to climb onto the raft. Jimmy pushed him off the raft. Caught up in the moment, with everyone hollering, splashing, and trying to dethrone Jimmy, no one noticed Ernesto sinking.

The cops took us in and questioned us individually. I was twelve at the time. For the next three days parents, police and just about the whole neighborhood gathered at the river. My mother was standing with Ernesto's mom when a police boat dragging the river found the body. As her son was being pulled from the river Mrs. Delgado let out the most horrific scream I had ever heard. I couldn't even look at her.

No one was blamed for Ernesto's drowning, but something ate away at my soul. Jimmy Stanton and I stayed friends but we both grew up drinking a lot. One night in a bar when we were in our twenties Jimmy told me he knew Ernesto couldn't swim. I asked him, "If you knew, why'd you push him off?" He looked at me, started crying and said, "I don't know. I swear to God, I just don't know."

Fun at the DMV
By John Maher

Last week my wife told me we need to renew our driver's licenses this year. Because of our age, we're in that dreaded demographic designation, Senior Citizen. We're required to retake the written exam, which adds insult to the indignity. The thought fills me with venom. I hate the DMV. Hate isn't powerful enough. Detest, despise, abhor; there aren't enough words that describe my deep abiding animus for this torture palace.

My judgments about the DMV are long-standing. They first surfaced on a Monday 57 years ago, the day after my 16th birthday. Like all the teenagers I knew, I had to get my learner's permit precisely on my 16th birthday. Since September 18th, 1960 fell on a Sunday, going to the DMV had to take place the very next day without question. Getting your learners-permit on your 16th birthday was an inalienable rite of passage for every teenager living in New York State. On the appointed day, I insisted that my mother pick me up at school and whisk me post-haste to the DMV in Mineola six miles away from my hometown.

Although my older brother Tom had briefed me about getting my learner's permit, thinking about the process produced sweaty armpits and jangled my nerves. My anxiety increased when I entered the DMV with my mother in tow and saw the overflow crowd of people. A sea of sullen faces loitered in messy lines that snaked all over the place. Other unfortunates sat in endless rows of painful plastic chairs waiting to be summoned to the counter. As a point of reference, this was the lone New York State DMV office for all of Nassau County. The County's 1960 population was 1.3 million people. To say the place was crowded would be an understatement.

My first DMV experience introduced me to the two issues that colored every later visit. I cannot discount the pain caused by the long lines or endless waiting. They're bad enough. It's the misery of dealing with brain-dead DMV clerks and the insufferable eye exam that get my back teeth grinding with dread.

Over the years, I've endured visits to DMV offices in four states. In some, the crowds were smaller and the wait less. But the clerks and the eye exam seemed the same. I am convinced that all DMV clerks must attend the same training school that teaches the three S's: Slow, surly and stupid. It doesn't matter if the DMV office is in New York, South Carolina, Massachusetts, or California, they're all the same. They process the paperwork at sloth speed, they are doing you a favor by their existence, and they have IQ's three points lower than a stapler. These attributes varied by office and state. It's a matter of degrees. But for the eye exam, they were all the same.

I've been hypersensitive about being blind in my right eye since I was little. I've always felt different, not entirely whole. My mother abetted these feelings. Soon after the doctors removed the eye when I was nine, my mother stated that my having one eye was a family secret. I was not to tell friends or schoolmates of my condition. It wasn't until 1999 after moving to California to take care of my 86-year-old mother I learned the reason for this family secret. During an intense conversation one afternoon she told me the deep-seated guilt she'd carried for 50 years. My mother blamed herself for my congenital cataract and eye surgery. She didn't want people to know what she believed was her responsibility.

Anything that brought unwanted attention to my having one eye sent me around the bend. The eye chart at the Mineola DMV that day in 1960 mortified and humiliated me. I had to explain to the cretin behind the counter why I couldn't see line #3 with my right eye. The mob behind me in line looked on with impatience. Every DMV visit after this where I had to read an eye chart dredged up the old bugaboo. Except for one episode that put the quietus to my sensitivity.

Since I planned on staying in California after I moved there in 1999 to take care of my 85-year-old mother, I needed a California driver's license. I drove over to the DMV office in Fountain Valley, the town next to Huntington Beach. The office was a one-story red brick nondescript building that belied its vast interior. On entering, lines meandered everywhere. Row after row of hard fiberglass chairs held disconsolate people looking like they were awaiting execution. There were no directional signs or information counter. A low hum of English, Spanish, and Vietnamese murmured voices competed with counter clerks barking "Next!" and "Step up!" and the regular timpani *blam, blam, blam* of smashing self-inking office stampers. I had arrived at Dante's ninth circle of hell, the one dealing with treachery.

I asked people in two different lines what that line did and at the third found it dispensed blank forms completed at standup shelves along the walls. Luckily, I had brought a pen. There were unfortunate others left adrift without writing implements; they're probably still there.

After a wait of 15 minutes, the gargoyle behind the counter informed me that reciprocity did not exist between California and Massachusetts. I couldn't just exchange my license. I was required to undergo a written exam and an eye test. Then she pushed the application forms at me and instructed, "Go over there, fill these out, and then get in that line there." She used her thumb to suggest a general direction further along the long counter where other misfortunate victims were filling out forms. As the heat of aggravation mushroomed, I repeated the Serenity Prayer several times in my head.

After a 20-minute wait in the second line, I arrived at the next hurdle. The garden gnome with coke-bottle glasses behind this counter seized my completed forms and scanned them without a greeting or a word. Then she looked through them again. And again. I was bemused that she took that amount of effort to check a dozen filled-in spaces on two pages. Satisfied, she shoved the forms back at me with a "Go over there" coupled with a chin move directing me toward a line down the counter. Like all the other lines in the building, it wound around an array of lanes fenced in by black cloth barrier tape stretched between stanchions.

After another interminable wait in a line of shuffling feet, I made it to the next position. Since patience and a capacity to tolerate stupid people are not in my family's DNA, on arriving at the counter, my mood was on a slow simmer. I was just this side of seething... at which point the broad-hipped troll behind the counter barked, "Step to your right, cover your right eye, and read line #3 with your left eye." And, so it began. Since I had my right eye removed, I'd worn an artificial eye. The current one was custom made, and you couldn't tell I was wearing a "glass eye." It was so well made that even doctors mistook it for a real eye. So, I covered my right nonsighted eye as instructed. Why confuse the woman right off? That would take place soon enough.

After rattling off lie #3 and line #2 to the counter lady's satisfaction, she again barked, "Cover your left eye and read line #3 with your right eye." I looked at her and replied, "That's not going to happen. I'm blind in my right eye." She scrunched up her face, squinted her eyes and glared at me with annoyance. Apparently, I was screwing up the routine and lo she would deal with this breach of procedures.

She reached under the counter, shuffled some paper, withdrew a form, and slammed it on the countertop. With the power of a very important person and peering at me down her nose, she announced, "Take this to an eye doctor. He needs to complete it." My mood shifted from frustrated bubbling anger to confusion. I said, "Why? Why do I have to have this filled out?" She studied me as if I were mentally disabled and said, "You need to have a doctor confirm your condition." My confusion morphed into the fourth stage of anger. I blew right past bothered, mildly irritated and agitated to indignant.

I took a deep breath and said, "I need a specialist to tell you I have one eye? I've told you I have one eye. Why would I come in here and lie about having one eye? What would be the benefit?" She ignored this with a dismissive expression and, "It's the rule."

I reached up with my right hand and removed the artificial eye from its socket. It's only held in place by the eyelids. Cupping it in my fist, I smashed it onto the countertop and opened my hand to display the eye face up. It lay there on the bare Formica surface looking forlorn but pristine and alive. Pointing at it, I said, "That's a glass eye. I am blind in my right eye." Seething and raising my voice, I pointed to the empty socket which drew her attention to it. I said, "That's an empty eye socket. There's no eye in there. I am not paying a specialist $200, so he can peer in here and tell me I'm missing my right eye."

The counter woman's face looked like someone having a stroke. Her eyes were as big pie plates, the sides of her face drawn in tight, and her mouth a constricted rictus line. People tell me I'm a scary looking person when I'm angry. I guess my Irish mug is partly to blame. To compound this, I weighed over 300 pounds, so I suppose my angry visage and size could be intimidating. Without equivocation, I can report that having an enraged, large, one-eyed man who's just plucked out his eye affected this woman. While I couldn't see them, I sensed the people in line behind me retreating like unarmed combatants or remora fish searching for a place to hide. They wanted no part in this action.

With her face frozen in mid-seizure, the counter woman barely audible said, "Wait here." No one remaining in the line behind me voiced any objection to the delay. She scurried over to a single plain grey metal office desk anchored in the vast sea of emptiness that encompassed the area behind the counters. At this desk sat a dark-haired middle-aged, bespectacled man. He was Jabba the Hutt's 2nd cousin or a distant relative. He didn't merely sit in his high-backed leather office chair. It was more like he had been poured into it.

The harried counter lady leaned into Jabba across the desk. With her palms planted on the desktop, elbows locked, shoulders tight, she reported her recent interactions with the incensed behemoth at her station. She delivered her summation with furtive looks in my direction, which prompted matching nervous glances from Jabba. After about 30 seconds of back-and-forth, the counter lady moved to Jabba's side of the desk where he pulled out an enormous white covered loose-leaf binder from a desk drawer. This tome had to be a foot thick. It was the most massive loose-leaf binder I had seen. Ever.

The pair turned pages in rapid succession, jumping from section to section, ostensibly looking for a relevant DMV regulation or directive that would tell them how to deal with an angry one-eyed man. Then Jabba closed the tome with finality, and the counter woman hustled back to her station at the counter. With her head drawn back from her shoulders and her chin tucked, face tight with repressed panic and trying to maintain composure, she said, "Please go over there and take your written test. Then come back here." A slight head nod to the left suggested I move to the testing position down the counter.

My mood had changed. The anger dissipated, replaced by an internal smiling gratification. Regardless of the outcome, I had won. At least on this day, I had successfully explained to a DMV ninny why I can't read an eye chart with my right eye.

When I arrived at the testing area, I found the counter person there very accommodating. I surmised she had heard my bellowing and demonstrative explanation. I also figured she saw the other counter lady's reaction. Her expression told me she understood clearly that I had one eye, that I was not at all happy with the DMV, and her best interests would be met by quickly administering the written exam.

I passed the written test, had my mugshot taken, and got my license. I had won, proof of the adage, "The squeaky wheel gets the grease," especially if you have one eye and weight 300 pounds.

The Role of Trees in a World of Torture
By Dan Dražen Mazur

LIKE MOST PEOPLE, I also immensely dislike children. This uneasiness is primarily caused by not knowing if the little brat you are dealing with is to become a good-natured tree hugger with the beard and body volume Santa could be jealous of—or grow up into a menacing skinny person with tiny mustache, ridden by an inferiority complex, raging testosterone, and ruthless egocentric personality, known simply as baby Adolf. The early signs of future behavior are highly unreliable, and the following story might illustrate this.

It was one regular Sunday, the day after Saturday, when little Josef discovered a plot. He was a withdrawn child, quiet and immersed into his own fantasies, who never caused much trouble to his parents. His hair was strong and plentiful, and his eyes were radiating curiosity and intelligence.

The Dzhugashvili family would come to the city park every summer Sunday as usual, where his parents would spend some time enjoying the afternoon shade and talking nonsense. Joseph could filter out their yapping by watching birds and squirrels, and by trying to figure out their everyday doings, and guessing why they are alive.

That fateful Sunday Joseph noticed that the tree normally growing straight across the bench his family usually occupied, was no longer there. Naturally, one would think that the tree was cut down and removed for whatever reason. However, there was another, completely mature tree at the same place where the old tree was, which was odd. Josef remembered that the missing tree had one big branch growing horizontally out of its main trunk, high above the ground, and leaned directly over their bench, providing pleasant shade for the people underneath. The current tree was also quite big and tall, but its branches reached out at an angle, going straight upwards, nothing like the tree Joseph remembered.

Joseph kept this discovery to himself but made sure to remember what the tree which replaced the original tree looked like, hoping when they visit, the old tree would be neatly back in its place. Joseph thought maybe 'his' tree had been taken to be repaired, and another one was put temporarily in its place, not to cause disturbance, panic, or protests of sensitive park visitors. Typical thinking of a kid his age.

Next Sunday Joseph realized that the tree that was there replacing the original tree was also no longer there, but was replaced by another one, even skinnier and taller. The Sunday after there was another tree there, replacing the one that replaced the one which replaced the original one. Surprised and disturbed more than ever, Joseph began observing other trees in the park more carefully, and to his amazement discovered that his original tree didn't disappear, instead, it was relocated and now growing toward the edge of the park. Joseph was sure this was 'his' tree, recognizing the horizontal branch. The second replacement tree was also found but relocated on the other side of the park.

Although young for his age, Joseph realized that these trees were so huge that relocating them regularly around the park must have been a monumental task for which many people and heavy machinery had to be involved.

Curious as he was, the Sunday after, Joseph brought with him crayons and marked the five trees around the bench with numbers, 1, 2, 3, 4, 5. His tactic was to mark the tree closest to their bench with number 1, next closest with number 2, and so forth.

Next Sunday, Joseph's suspicion was confirmed as he determined that the trees marked with 1, 2, 3, 4 and 5 were at their new locations, namely 3, 4, 5, 2, 1, using the same method of counting. The trees 5, 2, and 1 were moved completely outside of the original distances, while 3 and 4 were further away from their bench, and replaced with trees from different park areas, that Joseph didn't get to mark yet. To figure out if there was a pattern in these trees rotating was confusing and difficult, impossible.

One would think that frustrated Joseph would share his discovery with his parents, but he kept the revelation to himself. He was never compassionate about his parents, finding them boring and a nuisance. As much as it was irritating, his inability to figure out what was going on, he also felt triumphant - somebody was regularly rotating trees around the park, and nobody but him seemed to be noticing that.

As Joseph was growing up, he never forgot this, and years later, when his position allowed him, he ordered an investigation regarding the rotating trees. Unfortunately, it showed no results.

"Comrade Stalin, here is the investigation report. I am afraid we couldn't determine how it was possible to rotate the trees. We actually concluded this wasn't possible."

"Are you insinuating that I am a liar?!" Joseph yelled and jumped from his chair. He was upset because earlier that morning he discovered an unacceptable pimple on his forehead.

"Of course not, comrade Stalin. I'm just saying you were a boy then. Your imagination was vivid. We were simply unable to figure out what had happened," the man said, barely able to keep the contents of his intestines inside.

"We have determined that around that time a new town manager was hired, but we couldn't find any connection between this fact and the tree rotations."

"I want to see that man!" Joseph ordered, returning to the safety of his chair.

His order couldn't be fulfilled because the man had been dead for a decade, so Joseph never found a definitive answer to this mystery. Upset, Joseph ordered the disrespectful comrade who dared to question his honesty, be sentenced to the gulag. This bothered him quite a lot, but it also remains unknown how much this event contributed, if at all, to the world's history of tyranny.

When my mother told me this story I couldn't rest and find peace because of the mystery. Due to circumstances beyond my control, I was given the opportunity to go through the archives of the park and recreation department. I found out a simple answer to the mystery. That new director who took up the park manager position before the rotation of the trees had begun, had been the manager of a huge automobile tire shop where rotating of automobile tires was an everyday routine. He must have continued the practice out of the habit.

Now you know why I'm leery of being around children.

"Who's to say that dreams and nightmares aren't as real as the here and now?"—John Lennon

Genesis
By Gretchen Brinck

STARS FLARED OVERHEAD, then vanished like bright pebbles flung into a river. Jenna scooted deeper into her sleeping bag. It smelled of smoke, pitch, pine needles, clean dirt, sweat.

It smelled of Drake.

Here, where trees stopped growing and craggy slopes angled toward the mountain top, she could feel his ropy arms around her and his wispy beard against her neck. They'd always made love when they camped in the wilderness.

Directly above her, something else burst into flame, so close she could hear its small whoosh over the treetops. The ground shuddered when it hit beyond the fire pit. Multicolored flames darted out. Then darkness. Then a dull glow like an unquenched ember.

Jenna struggled into her jeans and boots. If the trees started burning, she'd have a dicey time escaping down the steep mountain trail.

But nothing caught fire. She huddled again in the sleeping bag and stared at the knot of shimmering heat.

Drake would have loved this experience. She'd done the right thing, climbing to this lonely, wild place for remembrance. The funeral had been nothing but a stage on which friends portrayed melodramatic grief. "Oh, Jenna," Drake's trekking buddy Ben had moaned to her turned back, "I was right beside him when ... there was nothing I could do. God!" He'd given a little sob. "At least let me return his backpack to you." He'd forced his card between her clenched fingers. "Call me when you're ready."

Ready for what? To learn how a skilled hiker like Drake could fall from a Himalayan trail and die?

"Look at that thing," she whispered to Drake in her mind. The fallen star throbbed redly till the moon sank toward morning.

When dawn woke her, she saw a small crater at the tree-line. The meteorite's flames had left glittery trails across the dirt.

Her boots crunched as she approached. Up close the burn lines glistened like mercury. A few feet below the crater's lip lay a black stone the size of a baseball.

Jenna's chunk of outer space, part shiny, part dull, glinting with crystal or mica, couldn't be less like a mega-ton, dinosaur-killing asteroid. It was just an ugly little rock.

Still, she used a roll of film on the scene when the sun rose higher, though Drake, not she, had been the expert at nature photography.

Sunday night Jenna made her long drive back to the overpopulated San Francisco Bay Area. At work on Monday, she robotically performed administrative tasks for computer nerds, but Drake and the meteorite crowded her attention. When she surfed the net that night, she learned that few human beings had ever witnessed an actual fall. She downloaded images of recovered meteorites. None matched hers. The known ones were "interplanetary." Was hers different because its origins were farther away -- intergalactic?

Scientists would go crazy over it.

"Yo!" Drake shouted in her head, and she saw the giant footprint they'd once come upon while cross-country skiing. Drake had raised his gloved fist. "Yo, Sasquatch! Head for the high country, Dude! Stay a mystery!"

Scientists would lock her meteorite into a chamber, chip it, zap it with x- and other rays, microscopically examine it, burn it with chemicals and argue over it in esoteric journals. Yo, Drake.

She told no one.

Saturday, she returned to the wilderness and struggled for hours up the deer trail to the tree-line.

Something had happened around the crater. Small mounds had erupted along the burn lines as if the mercury-like stuff had bubbled. Jenna came close. An inch high and an inch across, the gray-green lumps had smooth surfaces except for minute clefts across their tops. Jenna touched the bottom edge of the nearest one. The surface gave beneath her finger like firm flesh.

Of course. The things were just succulents. But how could they grow at this high altitude, in barely cooled intergalactic lava?

She couldn't stop gazing at hers, as she already considered the one she'd touched. Utterly minimalist, yet pregnant with possibilities, like the round end of a fertile egg. A cell about to divide. A mushroom cap concealing spores. A baby's bottom. A female mound.

The head of a male organ.

What? Tears burst from her eyes. This stupid nothing of a plant had struck her deepest wound. She and Drake had planned to have children soon.

Chilly drops hit her face. She stalked away to set up her rain tarp.

In the morning the succulents shone with raindrops. Jenna watched herself gently scoop hers up along with its soil and metallic particles. Drake had never taken anything from the wild nor left anything behind. He'd even packed out used Band-Aids and toilet paper.

But I just have to have this succulent, she told him, or his spirit, though she couldn't say why.

At home, she planted it in an artsy cappuccino mug and set it on the kitchen windowsill. Her orange cat, Muffin, sniffed it and then stepped over it, draping it with filaments of fur.

The following weekend Jenna boxed up the slim photo-essay nature books on which she and Drake had collaborated. She'd collect their royalties, but without Drake's beautiful photographs to inspire her, she doubted she'd write copy again. She paused over a studio portrait of his fascinating Asian-Polynesian face. Packed it with the books.

Then she watered the succulent. When she gave it a quarter turn, she noticed a lentil-sized, pale orange blemish on its lower edge.

Was the plant multiplying or did it have a fungus? She squinted. The bump seemed textured and no, this couldn't be. She rummaged through drawers for a magnifying glass and looked again.

The orange growth, wearing an expression of fat-cheeked contentment, was Muffin.

"Oh, God! Kitty kitty?"

Muffin bumped his forehead against her shin and rumbled.

Jenna picked the magnifying glass back up. Muffin's minute replica appeared solid and furry and three-dimensional. Was it moving? She couldn't tell.

"How did you do that?" she asked the plant, but as she spoke, she remembered Muffin draping fur across it. She plucked one of her own reddish-brown hairs and set it on the succulent's tiny cleft.

In the morning a dot had appeared next to Muffin's image. Jenna checked it morning and evening for days before it was large enough to be examined through the magnifying glass.

She saw herself: a lean, naked woman with reddish brown hair. "Oh, wow!" Jenna's delight bordered on love.

Could the succulent extrapolate images from sources other than hair? And would it accept flora as well as fauna? In her patio outside the window, pots and planter boxes burst with spring blooms. Jenna picked a purple petunia blossom and dropped it on the cleft. A pin-sized purple outcropping rewarded her in the morning. She tried the root of a cyclamen bulb. That worked too. When she gave the succulent an ant, the bug scuttled away instantly, yet next morning another tiny bump emerged.

Jenna squatted by the windowsill. "OK," she said. "You use lots of sources and you capture a being the second you touch it." Her eyes traveled over its round shape. A lot of space waited to be filled.

On her next free day, Jenna offered, in one hour, a chrysanthemum leaf, fresh tomato pulp, a feather, an orange peel, an onion skin, a garlic clove, a coffee bean and her favorite yellow petunia. In the morning she found a multitude of new bumps. She could hardly bear the long wait till she could capture them in the magnifying glass.

In addition to the plants, the succulent had replicated an aphid, a bird mite, a hummingbird, a ladybug, a tomato worm, whitefly, a fungus and weird things she didn't recognize but which must be microbes or mitochondria or bacteria or nematodes.

But she couldn't find the yellow petunia. "You don't take the same species twice?" Jenna returned to her patio and collected seventy-two more samples of plants, bugs, and worms.

On Monday she called in sick and foraged neighborhood flowerbeds and vegetable gardens, then gathered urban wildlife droppings from a shrubby vacant lot. It took hours to give the plant all the new offerings.

In the morning, when she'd seen the dozens of new outcroppings on the Mound, Jenna packed trail mix, juice, a thermos of coffee and her sleeping bag and headed for Golden Gate Park. She stepped from a sidewalk into the Park's dense, varied growth and plucked twigs, leaves, droppings, and insects. When darkness fell she switched on her flashlight and continued till she dropped asleep beneath a eucalyptus. She woke chilled with fog, ate a handful of trail mix, and kept going. She didn't go home till the trail mix had been gone awhile, didn't realize she'd been collecting for seven days till she checked the date on her computer.

When she finished giving Golden Gate Park to the plant, pinpoint dots completely covered its surface except the hairline cleft on top.

But if the Mound was full, why did Jenna still feel empty? "We've barely begun," she pleaded. "There's so much more I can give you." Something went wrong with her eyes. She squinted through the magnifying glass but could no longer see the dots. They had vanished into their gray-green landscape as she spoke.

The plant had made room for more.

"Why?" she asked, though till now the question hadn't occurred to her. "What will you do with them?" She set it on the floor, sat lotus style and gazed down at it till it blocked out the walls, the kitchen, the wind blowing through the window. Jenna did not know if it was day or night when she sank into sleep.

In her dreams, she glimpsed a gray-green planet through clouds. She descended to its surface, which held only dirt and lichen and pure, swift rivers. She and Drake plucked sparkling stones from a riverbed and threw them over their shoulders. From her first stone sprang a brilliant blue kingfisher, from Drake's a drooping willow. Jenna's second stone created a leaping trout and Drake's stone created a brown bear. Jenna opened her eyes to her moonlit kitchen. She understood.

The Mound was gathering life for a clean new planet and she'd been appointed its life-giving goddess.

At sunrise, she drove to work and packed her things. Her boss Arnold, sleeping beneath his desk as computer nerds are wont to do, woke and leaned in her doorway, running his fingers through his unwashed hair. "You look terrible," he told her between yawns. "You shouldn't make life-changing decisions while you're grieving."

"Grieving?" Pain over Drake had shrunk like the replicas on the plant.

She sublet her apartment to a desperate college student and dropped Muffin off with a cat-loving friend. Then she loaded Drake's old van with clothes, cameras, camping gear, credit cards and the plant and headed for the coast. She slept next to the highway above a rocky beach.

At dawn she tucked the succulent into a net shopping bag. She'd take it to the samples, not the samples to it. Dangling the bag from her wrist, she scrambled over slimy rocks to the tidal pools.

With every wave, fleshy plants opened and closed like mouths seeking the multitude of tiny life forms. Even the slime Jenna skidded over was vibrantly alive. "So amazing," she told the plant, dropping sample after sample into the bag on top of it. "You'll love this."

Cold water crashed over her head. She fell sideways. The wave tumbled her over barnacle-covered rocks, then dumped her on the beach and fled. Its rushing wake sucked the bag out with it. Moments later the bag reappeared in the rising curve of the next wave, crashed on the shore, rode away again with the undertow. Jenna plunged into the surf after it. Her mouth filled with gritty seawater. She dove through the next breaker and swam out.

Filthy with seaweed and foam, the bag floated on the swells as if waiting for her. She kicked her way to it, tied it to her wrist and let the waves wash her to shore like driftwood.

The cappuccino cup and metallic dirt were gone, but the succulent lay tangled in the bottom of the bag. Its gray-green skin had gone blotchy and was streaked with sand and salt. It looked sick.

Jenna untangled it and held it gently. Tears ran down her cheeks. "Don't die," she pleaded. But how could the plant and the replicas survive a half hour in the salty ocean?

The plant nestled easily in her palm. Its flat underside had no roots. She faced the fact she'd been avoiding: the Mound was no more a succulent than the space rock was a meteorite. It was a womblike vessel incubating strings of DNA for the clean, pure planet she'd seen in her dream.

Jenna rinsed the mound in a drinking fountain by the parking lot. Then she set it in the van's window. The mottled surface slowly coarsened into pinpricks.

In the morning she bought a series of microscope lenses and a tweezer-like holder. Through one she examined the mound's surface. Sea life sprang into view: a seal, sea lion, fish, whale, dolphin, shrimp, plankton. The mound had taken full advantage of the sea water's animal excrement and sperm, plant spores, and all other traces of life. Far from destroying the Mound and its DNA, immersion had proved a shortcut.

She jotted a quick plan: she'd travel north during summer, and by late fall would head south, and in addition to here and now life forms, she would give some extinct species a chance for new life in her little world.

She taped the plan to the dashboard, started the ignition and lost track of time. Nothing mattered anymore except collecting life. She took the mound everywhere with her in its net bag. It plunged into rivers, lakes, swamps, was dragged through the underbrush of forests; it absorbed desert microbes, bone dust from long-extinct creatures, pollen from rare plants Jenna located on heritage farms, dung and guano from zoos. It dangled from her arm as she swam with seals in the Galapagos Islands and when she hiked in a protected Amazon rainforest rich with exotic and endangered species.

And every night when she was alone, she cupped the mound --by now swollen as if pregnant -- and, using ever stronger lenses, plunged into her created world. Its scenes endlessly fascinated her yet remained endlessly incomplete.

One evening she pulled up the van in Puerto Natales in Chile. In a day or two she'd take a bus to the spectacular national park, Torres del Paine. She lit her lamp, held the mound and picked up the strongest lens.

And saw only gray-green.

Where were her lovely forests and animals, her resurrected extinct species, her exotic crops? She ran her finger lightly over the mound's surface. It felt grainy. Through the lens she watched a green dot appear and resolve into a scraggy pine tree. Next to it a flesh-colored pinprick emerged: herself.

Terrible emptiness opened within her. "Not yet," she pleaded. Jenna turned tear-filled eyes to the calendar she'd taped to the van's wall. Yesterday must have been Sunday; locals had thronged the churches. She pulled an ATM receipt from her purse. March 27, it said. Three days ago.

She felt as if she were swimming up from murk into fresh air. Drake had died a year ago today. His funeral had been held two weeks later, April 14. That meant the space rock fell into her life on the 15th.

Could she make it to the California mountainside in two weeks? Battered by a year of rough travel and minimal maintenance, the van barely ran. She'd spent chunks of her dwindling funds on jury-rigged repairs.

She packed her few worthwhile possessions, sold the van to a pair of guides cheap, and used her last shred of credit for an airplane ticket.

On the way to the airport she made the cab driver stop twice so she could pick interesting roadside grasses for the mound.

During the all-night flight, she leaned her head against the cold window and clutched the net bag as her recurring dream came. She and Drake threw bright stones that became living beings as they hit the ground.

She woke gasping. How would the recreated life forms propagate if the mound collected only a single sample of each one?

She took the mound into her palm. The mushroom cap, a dividing cell, the female organ, the rounded half of a fertile egg. There had been at least thirty mounds at the crater. She visualized one merging with hers, each with its own load of DNA.

But hers carried richer treasure than the others. What could they collect up there at the tree-line except a pine tree, a few seeds dropped by passing birds, maybe a drift of pollen or feathers? No humanity.

When she arrived in the San Francisco airport, she hurried to a pay phone and dug out her long-forgotten address book. "Ben?"

"Jenna? God, where did you disappear to? Your boss said . . ."

"Come get me. Bring Drake's back pack."

"Well, sure, but are you all right? You sound . . ."

She forced herself to be patient. Months had passed since she'd spoken to a human being for any purpose other than achieving access to an offering for the mound. "I'm sorry, Ben, I'm weirded out from jet lag. I was in Patagonia."

She waited for him outside the terminal, shivering in fog. He pulled up in a vintage VW bus and jumped out. "Jenna?"

"Yeah."

"Is that all your luggage?"

"Luggage?" She hefted her backpack and Guatemalan shoulder purse, lifted the net bag on her wrist, then caught the expression on Ben's face. "What's wrong?" she asked.

"You look so different."

She leaned toward the VW's side mirror and saw weathered features and long, knotted hair.

Later she'd have time to care. Not now. "You brought Drake's pack?"

"It's at my place," said Ben. She'd forgotten how his eyes smiled through his wire-framed glasses.

He took her to an old Victorian house in San Francisco where he had a three-room apartment filled with color. For curtains and bedspread, he used brilliant Indian tapestries, and he'd covered the walls with his own travel photos, prayer flags and baskets. Incense burned in a metal holder.

He made her shower and work tangles out of her hair while he prepared rice, vegetable curry and a fruit and yogurt dessert. On the way to his kitchen, wearing his robe and dangling the net bag from her wrist, she gave the mound a thread from a wall hanging she suspected contained yak wool; then she added a bit of ash from the incense. She fell asleep over the fourth bite of rice and woke late the next morning beneath a patchwork quilt on the couch. "I'm at work," said the note on his refrigerator. "Back at 5:30."

In his closet she found Drake's back pack. State-of-the-art when he bought it, its light-weight, waterproof fabric was torn now and stained with ground- in mud. Himalayan mud? She scraped a bit and gave it to the mound before she opened the pack's clasps and buried herself in Drake's familiar possessions, baggy tan shorts loaded with pockets, his favorite old jersey, blue jeans worn soft with age, his battered down jacket and hiking boots, a crumpled shaving kit, though he'd seldom needed to shave.

The zipped inner pocket of the pack held what she was looking for: a plastic bag of used Band-Aids spotted with Drake's blood. She dropped them into a bowl of cold water, and when the water turned pink she dropped the mound into it. She was white, he was Asian and Polynesian. Would the mound consider him different enough from her to be a sample?

She cleaned everything up and climbed back under the quilt with the mound in its net bag. When Ben came home, she borrowed money from him. "Will you be back?" he asked, his eyes sad behind his glasses.

She leaned into him, slid her arms around him. More than a year had passed since she'd last embraced a human being. Warm and nice, yes, but still an intrusion. "See you later, I think."

She caught a Greyhound bus and made it up to the tree-line at dusk on April 14th.

Sticks, bits of fur and feathers, rotting meat, maggots and flies and other debris surrounded the crater. She had to scrape it away with sticks to get at the mounds. To the naked eye their surfaces seemed as smooth as the first time she'd seen them, but like hers, they had grown.

A fox trotted across the dirt as if she weren't there and dropped a small rodent onto one of the mounds. Then he lay down inches away with his chin on his paws and stared intently at his gray-green lump, nose twitching, ears lifting. She suspected the animal's rapt expression matched her own when she studied her mound through a microscope lens.

What fascinated the fox so much? Fox pheromones? Scents of the hunt? Jenna realized she wasn't a life-giving goddess, mother of all living things in a tiny world. Like the fox, she'd been seduced and enslaved. And for what?

Suppose instead of populating a new planet, the mounds' creators subjected earth's life forms to cruel experiments in some floating, alien lab? Jenna strode to the fire pit, and when she forced the damp wood finally to catch, she studied the flames. Should she entrust the mound with the thousands and thousands of DNA strands she'd given it, or should she burn it?

Imagine giving these wondrous life forms a chance in a clean, pure place. If it existed.

She lit her lantern and pulled out her best lens. She trained it on the mound.

Against the gray-green backdrop, perfectly formed, stood Drake's replica. Her own emerged, its hand touching Drake's. Gradually flora and fauna came into view around them, not static but in motion. Trees and grasses swayed in invisible winds. Ancient and modern crops grew, animals browsed. She and Drake walked in a vivid rain forest swarming with life.

Let it be true.

Jenna took the mound to the crater and set it with the others. Then she climbed into her sleeping bag and waited.

Long into the night, the rock in the crater began to glow like an ember. It shimmered, then briefly shot out flaming arms. Their flash of light revealed the mounds flattening as they released their cargo to the rock. Jenna jumped when the tiny stars burst across the sky. Her rock shot up from the ground and streaked across the treetops. When it joined the others, she lost sight of which glittering speck was hers and she realized what a wealth of earth life the group must have gathered. They flared, then vanished like bright pebbles into a river flowing to a distant soil.

Bob Matthews
By Roger Antony

BOB SAT ALONE in the dimly lit movie theater with what looked like a nearly full bag of popcorn propped up in his lap.

In a few moments, the cleaning crew would come in and sweep the aisles removing any discarded bags, boxes and drink cups before the next showing. Bob had watched the movie twice already. After each show, he would leave, duck into the men's room then return just as the lights were dimming and the preview of coming attractions were starting.

The bag of popcorn was just a prop. He had eaten all but a few popped kernels during the first show. What few kernels he hadn't eaten he spilled out into a napkin after everyone had exited the first show. He used napkins and stuffed them into the bottom of the popcorn bag, then put the popcorn back in the bag. One would think he had a nearly full bag of popcorn. This was what he wanted people to think as he sat through the second and third shows.

He spent most Saturdays away from home, as far away from home as he could get without a car. Some Saturdays he spent at the library, some he would walk through the woods to the Army base nearby where his father worked and watch the soldiers march. When he had the money, he'd go to the movies.

Bob's father was a captain on the base. He was in charge of the drill sergeants and had more than two hundred fifty men beneath him. Bob's father was a mean man like all the drill sergeants. At home, he seldom spoke to Bob or Bob's mother with compassion or understanding. It was always an order: do this, do that.

On weekends it was particularly bad since his father got drunk every Friday night after leaving the base and barely sobered up by Monday morning. Those were the hours that Bob stayed away from home. Sometimes he stayed away until Sunday evening, leaving his mother home alone with his father.

From past experience, Bob knew that if his father got drunk before dinner on Friday night, the weekend would be bad. Bob either made arrangements to sleep over a friend's house on Saturday night or took his sleeping bag, which he kept in the garage alongside a small duffel bag, to the local park to sleep.

The park contained four ballfields fanning out from a small clubhouse containing a concession stand and a public restroom, which was kept unlocked year-round.

Tall pine trees surrounded the park on two sides. Running through the pines on the east-side was Silver Creek, a tributary of the Argyle River.

Five years ago, when Bob was only nine he spent a lot of time in the park along the creek. The water was teaming with life, from spiders gliding on the surface of the water, to guppies in the pooled areas, to frogs and snakes at the water's edge.

Bob no longer spent time capturing guppies to take home and show his mother. Now he used the park as a weekend retreat from his father's abuse. He tolerated his father during the week when he was sober. During the week, his father would have a couple of beers after dinner. On weekends his father would get drunk and mean. That's when Bob made sure that he was away from home.

The theater manager signaled the start of the next show by dimming the lights. A few seconds later the speakers came alive and the screen displayed brilliant colors and the coming attractions. Coming attraction previews lasted ten minutes. Bob had timed the two earlier showings. He waited until it was a few minutes before the end of the coming attractions before he flushed the toilet, washed his hands and left the restroom carrying what appeared to be a full bag of popcorn.

He found a seat in the back of the theater this time. For the first showing, he sat near the front of the theater. During the second showing, he sat in the center of the middle aisle halfway back from the screen. It was his favorite location. For the third showing, he found a seat in the back row adjacent to the wall.

Bob loved movies and when he was old enough he wanted to move to California and write for the movies. He was certain of that. In fact, he had started writing a movie script based upon his life.

For now, he kept the names of the real people in his story. He had already selected who would play the parts in his movie. Ernst Borgnine would play his father, Eugene Matthews. Donna Reed would play his mother, Margaret. A new young actor needed to play him. Bob was thinking of James Dean or Vince Edwards. Either would do, but he favored James Dean because he felt that he looked a lot like James Dean.

The third show let out just after six-thirty. He waited until everybody had left before leaving his seat. He left the phony bag of popcorn on the floor, then walked to the front of the theater and exited. He normally left through one of the exits near the screen rather than exit back into the theater lobby where he might be seen by the theater manager or friends.

Bob squinted as he opened the door, the sun still bright in the sky on this early June evening. He pulled his ball cap down across his forehead keeping his eyes shaded from the sun. He had several choices: go home and eat with his parents or buy a hamburger at the Dairy Queen two blocks away. Either way, he'd have to go home to pick up his sleeping bag.

His father had gotten drunk early on Friday night, a bad omen. Bob was certain that he'd be meaner than hell if he showed up for dinner.

He jingled the three-quarters in his pocket, enough for a drink and a hamburger. He made his decision to eat at the Dairy Queen then sneak into the garage and get his sleeping bag. He was about to cross the street when a large hand was planted firmly on his shoulder.

Before he had a chance to turn around, he heard his father's slurred voice, "Son, where you been?"

Bob turned to face his father, a tall, lean forty-two-year-old man with short cropped blond hair, wearing a green Army tee shirt, khaki pants, and black highly polished military boots and devoid of a smile.

"I've been at the movies, sir."

"Your mother's been wondering where you've been," he said.

"I told her I'd be gone all day."

Eugene Matthews' eyes were partially glazed from too much Jack Daniels. His father usually started with beer. If he wanted to get drunk, which was his standard operating procedure on Friday night, he'd switch to Jack Daniels. A few shots of Jack and he was buzzing. A few more shots, he'd get abusive. A few more and he'd get meaner than hell.

Margaret would go upstairs to the bedroom and get in bed and try to go to sleep. Even if she wasn't asleep when Eugene came in she would fake it. He could be really abusive if he found her awake.

Sometimes in a drunken stupor, he would stare down at her in bed and cuss at her. Sometimes he would turn around and go back downstairs and fall asleep in front of the television. However, most nights he would shake her until she woke and then tell her how old she looked, or how she couldn't fix a good meal or whatever negative thought came into his inebriated mind. He might even slap her.

Bob could hear his father's voice through the walls of the upstairs bedroom. He often heard his mother pleading with his father to stop hurting her. At times he felt he should go into his parent's room and protect his mother, but he never did. His father was a big man. When he was drunk, he seemed to get stronger and more fearless.

Bob used to lock his door to escape his father's tyranny, but his father had busted his door lock more than six months ago to get in and spread disapproval and discontent with his son. The lock didn't keep his father out that night and now that the casing around the strike had been damaged; it would no longer lock.

Bob spent most Friday and Saturday nights away from home, but his mother had no choice. She had to stay at home. She endured his father's invectives and diatribes.

Eugene grabbed his son's upper arm and said, "Son, let's go home."

"I don't want to go, sir."

"What do you mean you don't want to go?" His father's slurred voice taking on a hard edge as he held on to his son's arm.

"Let go. You're hurting me," Bob said.

"I'm going to hurt you more if you don't come along," he said.

At fourteen and six feet three inches tall, Bob was three inches taller than his father, but forty pounds lighter. Without realizing it he pulled his arm free from his father's grasp and said, "No, I'm not coming home."

"You're coming with me, you little piece of shit," said Eugene reaching for his son's arm only to find air. Bob had turned and was running down the street.

Eugene gave chase for fifty or sixty feet then stopped, put his head down and puked on the sidewalk. People nearby looked at the hunched over man as vomit splattered on his polished boots and pant legs.

Bob knew he was well ahead of his father, so he stopped and looked back. He saw his father bent over discharging food and bile onto the sidewalk while others stared at his father wondering whether or not to call for help.

Eugene rose unsteadily and looked at his only son. "You son of a bitch," he yelled, then with his left-hand wiped vomit from his lower lip and repeated, "you son of a bitch."

Bob watched his father turn and slowly saunter away. At that pace, it would take his father at least fifteen minutes to get to their house. Bob turned the corner and started jogging. He could be home in less than five minutes. He needed to check on his mother before his father got home.

Mrs. Matthews turned from washing dishes in the sink as her son entered the back door. "You okay?" She asked.

Bob waited a moment to catch his breath. "Dad tried to drag me home."

"What?"

"He met me in front of the movie theater and grabbed me. He wanted me to come home."

"I'm sorry Bob. Your father's drunk again. He's not himself."

"He's always drunk and he's coming home. He's mean tonight," Bob said looking at a reddish blue bruise forming on the right side of his mother's cheek. "Did he do that to you?"

"It's not bad," she said.

"It's not bad? You say that every time. He shouldn't hit you. He's your husband, not your master."

"Don't worry son."

"Mom, I do worry. He's going to be home in a few minutes. I'm not going to be here. We ought to call the police. He needs help."

"Don't Bob. It'll ruin his military career."

"So, we have to accept his drinking because of his career. How about our lives? Aren't we supposed to have lives without fear or abuse? My friends have fathers in the military and they don't get drunk and hurt their family."

"Bob, your father has a problem."

"I know he has a problem. He needs help." Bob looked at his watch. It was nearly fifteen minutes since he had left his father. "What are you going to do, Mom?"

"Nothing," she said while drying the last plate with a towel.

"Well, that's great. I'm leaving."

"Bob don't go. I need you here."

"So, he can hit me like he hit you?"

"He won't do that to you. He loves you."

"He loves me. Yeah, right. He loves me so much that he gets drunk." He paused then added, "Is that right? Am I missing something? Dad needs help."

"He knows that."

"Then why doesn't he get it?"

As Margaret said, "I don't know," the front door opened. A few moments later Eugene walked through from the dining room.

He stared at his wife and son. "I see you've come home," Eugene said with a menacing tone.

"That's right. I wanted to make sure Mom was okay."

"Your mother's fine," said Eugene.

"Yeah, if you forget about the big bruise on her face," said Bob.

"Yeah, your mother deserved it."

"Really, I guess beating up on little women shows your strength. Is that it?" Bob said taunting his father.

"You smart ass," said Eugene.

"Why don't you pick on someone your own size?"

"You mean like you," Eugene said looking up at his son.

"Yeah, that's right. Me. I'm fourteen years old. I'm a real threat, right dad? I'm your enemy?"

Eugene stepped forward prepared to strike his son. Margaret turned to face her husband. "Eugene stop it. He's your son. You're drunk."

"Yeah, he's my son: smart ass fourteen-year-old."

"So, you intend to hurt me?"

"You're goddamn right, you smart ass."

"Eugene, don't you dare touch your son. Eugene, you hear me?"

Spitting out the words, he said, "I hear you, you old bitch."

As he lunged toward his son, Margaret grabbed a frying pan from the counter and swung it catching Eugene on the back of his head forcing him forward toward her son. Eugene collapsed into his son. Bob held him for a second before lowering him to the floor.

Margaret shocked by her actions stared down at her unconscious husband. She let the frying pan drop from her hands and stooped to her prostrate husband. Bob stood motionless, aware that his mother had protected him from his father and that she was now in mortal danger.

While she bent down and stroked her husband's head, Bob picked up the kitchen wall phone and dialed the Townsend City police. His mother looked at him as he spoke into the telephone and described to the dispatcher the circumstances.

Fifteen minutes later four policemen in two patrol cars arrived. Bob and his mother were sitting at the dining room table when the officers arrived. The screen door was unlocked, and Margaret told them to enter. The officers came through the door single file.

Two officers went into the kitchen where Eugene lay. One bent down and felt his pulse and put his ear adjacent to Eugene's mouth and nose and listened for any sound of breathing. The second policeman using a radio contacted dispatch and relayed the need for an ambulance.

Two of the four officers left before the ambulance arrived, the other two remained and interviewed Bob and his mother. Margaret had tears in her eyes as she answered the officer's questions including how she came by that bruise on her face. She knew that her statements would be used by the military to demote or discharge her husband. When the officers had completed the questioning of his mother, they turned to Bob and asked him whether he wanted to add anything to what his mother had said.

"No, sir."

"Ma'am, your husband needs help."

"I know," she said.

"Unless he gets help, there could be a repeat," said the officer doing most of the questioning.

Mrs. Matthews affirmed her understanding by shaking her head.

"Are you going to press charges, ma'am?"

"What do you mean?"

"Your husband has committed assault and battery. He can go to jail."

"Oh no, not jail."

"If you file charges, he'll serve some time, usually thirty days. It may make a difference."

"What difference would that be?" Margaret asked the officer.

"Your husband will know that he can't treat you that way without repercussions."

"But you don't have to live with him," she said, her face damp with tears.

"That's right, I don't. You and your son might want to move out at least for a while."

"Move where?"

"Ma'am, it's just a thought. It's entirely your decision. Just keep in mind that most abusers do not stop abusing until they're stopped."

Mrs. Matthews looked at her son then at the officers. "What does that mean?"

"Jail time," said an officer.

Bob turned to the officers. "I want to press charges. I want him to serve jail time. He deserves it."

"Are you sure?" The taller of the officers asked.

"Yes," said Bob. "I'm sure. Mom, it's for the good. Dad's been getting more violent every weekend."

After the ambulance carrying Eugene Matthews and the two officers left, Margaret and Bob sat in the dining room wondering whether or not they had done the right thing. Before departing, a police officer said that Eugene would probably be sober enough to be released on Sunday. "Being a military officer, he'd get bail without a hitch."

"I think we should move out tonight," said Bob.

"Move where?"

"What about Aunt Mary? She'll take us in. She's got room in her house."

"But she lives in Colorado. That's nearly four hundred miles away."

"Dad's going to be mad when he gets home."

"I can't leave your father."

"Do you love him? I mean really love him? He certainly can't love you, to hit you around like he's done for years."

"I'm not sure," she said. "How are we going to live?"

"We'll find a way."

"Are you sure?"

"I'm sure that Dad will be meaner than ever when he gets home. I don't think we want to be here."

Bob and his mother packed the family car with clothing and personal items. As a military family, they had moved a half-dozen times. This station was the longest for Eugene Matthews, five years next month.

It was nearly midnight by the time they finished packing. Bob locked the back door and checked throughout the house to make sure they had everything they needed. He had even crawled up into the attic to get their winter clothes. His mother grabbed all the pictures and the address and telephone directories. She was certain that when her husband found the house vacant, he would presume that she and Bob had taken off to be with a relative. He'd find their telephone numbers, but why make it easy for him.

Margaret took some cooking utensils and silverware, leaving Eugene enough to get along.

On the way out of town, she stopped at an ATM and took out the maximum amount. She'd do it again when they were in New Mexico and again in Colorado. There wasn't much in the account, but she'd get as much as she could.

Margaret's sister, Mary Anne, a seventh-grade teacher, lived alone in a three-bedroom townhome in Castle Rock, a town midway between Colorado Springs and Denver. Mary Anne, six years older than Margaret, had moved into the townhome almost four years ago with a boyfriend who left shortly afterward opting for a job in California.

His mother stopped at an exit along I-25 north of Santa Fe. Margaret debated whether or not to call her sister. They were five hours away. After debating the pros and cons, she dialed her sister.

The six o'clock call on Sunday morning woke Mary Anne from a sound sleep. Bob overheard his mother's side of the conversation and when she hung up she had a smile on her face.

"What did your sister say?" Bob asked.

"I woke her up. She wants us to come."

"Is that why you're smiling?"

"No. Mary Anne said that Eugene called her a half hour ago. She told him she hadn't heard from me in more than two weeks and if she did he'd be the last person she'd tell. He said he wanted me to come home. Mary Anne told him it was about time I left him. He called her a bitch, but she had the last word. She told him to go to hell and then hung up."

Bob was watching his mother intently, fearing she would start to cry, except she didn't cry. Instead, she wrapped her arms around her son's waist and smiled up at him. "If he'd left you alone I would've stayed."

"Mom, you shouldn't have put up with him."

"What was I supposed to do? You don't marry for better. You marry for better or worse."

"Mom, it couldn't get much worse. We made the right decision."

"You're probably right," said Mrs. Matthews.

"Mom, I am right," said Bob.

The Party
By Bill Lynam

MAC O'ROURKE PULLED HIS VOLVO up in front of the Victorian house with its two-story silo observatories, its crenelated scroll-work, and shingled-sided mansard roof and gawked at this mansion from a time. He pulled the doorbell that gave a faint ringing. Several minutes later, Geraldine Sommers answered and let him in. She knew he was coming. It was an insurance deal. The cops had already been there. What had gone on was over. Now, it was just the formalities. Paperwork.

"Come in Mr. O'Rourke," she chimed. He took off his fedora and put it on the sideboard.

"Come into the parlor. We can talk there. Would you like some tea?"

"No thanks just ate. Mind if I smoke?"

"Please do. Call me Gerry, Geraldine's too formal."

Geraldine, aka, Gerry, was one of two witnesses to the death of Hilda Hoover, owner of the house. The other witness, Brenda Postpistle, was in the hospital with a bullet wound. Gerry was at home where all three lived and Hilda was at the mortuary.

"Let's start from the beginning," Mac suggested.

"Us girls were having a party. You know? We had a little bubbly, actually, a lot.

When I woke up the next day, especially after the fire, the firemen, the cops and all; then I remembered Hilda was gone. She was sweet. So, yeah, we were partying when Brenda lit a cigarette, then fumbled it and dropped it on the bed and burned a hole in the sheets down to the mattress. Smoke started pouring out of the hole and nobody is really paying attention and whuff! up comes flames. Finally, we paid attention. Then, Hilda went over and was going to put out the fire, so she dumped half the bottle of brandy on the smoking hole in the bed. Shit! You can guess what that did. A fireball, more smoke and we all jumped off the bed as the sheets and mattress totally ignited and filled the room with smoke. Brenda got water and tossed it on the bed, then got some more. By then, the brandy burned out and the mattress was smoldering and stinking. There was still brandy left in the jug, so Hilda downed it, choked and I don't know if it was the liquor or the smoke. She looked kind of funny and went to get a cigarette. That's when it happened."

Gerry started crying and clamed up. I waited for a while then asked her if she wanted a glass of water or to sit down. Soon, she regained her composure, dried her eyes and continued with a little coaching.

"So, what went on next?" Mac asked.

"It was the cigarette lighter that did it." Gerry said. "It's shaped like a gun, almost like the derringer Hilda always carried. She was paranoid about strangers or something and only felt comfortable when she had her gun close by. When she pulled the trigger on the cigarette gun lighter, flame comes out of the end of the barrel. So, Hilda was half in the bag, woozy from either the smoke or the bubbly, she grabs a cigarette, fumbles for her cigarette lighter, gets her derringer instead, puts the cigarette in her mouth, aims the lighter at the end of the cigarette, pulls the trigger and no flame comes out, only a .223mm slug hits her cheek and blows out her brains on the left side of her head. When she fell, she still has the derringer in her hand and when she hit the floor, the two-shot gun went off and hit Brenda in the thigh or maybe it was her ass, I don't know for sure. She's in the hospital now. What a mess. Damn house is on fire, Hilda is mush and poor Brenda is screaming and bleeding. I'm holding my drink, smoking a doobie and baby, the party is definitely over."

"Where was the derringer that night?" Mac asked.

"On the dresser next to her lighter."

"Let's look in the bedroom. I'd need to see the scene and take photos."

Gerry pushed open the bedroom door after sweeping the crime-scene tape away the cops had put there. A fistful of stinky water, smoke, charred wood and soggy mattress hit our noses. Puddles of inky charcoal water spotted the floor. Mac looked over the bed, the dresser, the room and the carnage and took pictures. A wet piece of paper floated in a puddle. It looked official with a logo and said it was a receipt for an institutionalized…something or someone. Had more words but was waterlogged and bleeding ink. At the end, a signature by Dr. Joy L…and more wet smudge.

"You girls did a good job on this room," Mac said. "Gerry, you know Hilda took out a million-dollar life insurance policy four years ago. There'll be an investigation of her death. Keep the room locked. We'll have to go over it and gather evidence. And, we have to get Brenda's statement and the coroner's report before any decision is made on the policy."

Mac noticed there was no sign of the cigarette gun lighter in the room. Gerry had volunteered that the firemen had tossed the smoking mattress through the window and the cops had taken the derringer for ballistic tests.

At the hospital, Mac interviewed Brenda after finding her in room 232 on the second floor. She was lying in bed with IV tubes hooked to her and drains coming out of her raised, bandaged leg. She looked very uncomfortable propped up and watching a soap on the overhead TV.

"Brenda, I'm Mac O'Rourke from the Unlimited Life Insurance Company. I'm an investigator and need to talk to you about Hilda's death and the incident at your house. I hope this is a good time."

Without a pause, Brenda launched into her troubles. "That damn bullet hit my leg, went up my thigh and shattered my hip. Now they've got to dig it out and I have to have a hip replacement. How's that for dumb luck?" She went on for some time about her injury, her pain, what she was going to do, who she was going to sue, until finally, she focused on Mac and said, "Who are you and what do you want?"

"Brenda, you and Gerry are named as heirs to Hilda's estate in a million-dollar life insurance policy she took out."

"Yes, I know. We were partying last night because Hilda was just released after five years in the looney bin. She had a mental breakdown five or six years ago and after her family couldn't take care of her anymore, they sent her off to a private mental hospital for treatment. While she was there, Gerry and I lived in her house and took care of it, paid all the bills. Hilda was always saying she was going to end it. But, she never said what she was going to end. She was drinking a lot that night and seemed really happy. Sometime in the night, she snuggled up to me and whispered in my ear, giggling and said, 'They didn't let me out, I escaped.'"

"Poor Hilda. She was a good friend until she went around the bend," Brenda said.

"Thank you, Brenda, I believe I have all I need. But, do you know the name of hospital she was in?"

MEMO Case File 4326: In the matter of Hilda Hoover, age 32, deceased, of the address 458 Westchester Blvd., White Plains, NY, holder of Life Policy PO4738957394, dated August 4th, 1986, initiated by the same Hilda Hoover should be declared invalid, null and void as said policyholder on the date of the start of the policy date was being treated for drug and alcohol dependencies, depression and had made three previously unreported suicide attempts.

This recommendation is based on evidence of the subject's mental illness as substantiated by medical records subpoenaed from the files of Dr. Jerome Whittaker, her physician. Dr. Paul Hume, her psychiatrist, Dr. John Mercer, her analyst, medical records subpoenaed from the Bright Star Treatment Facility (enclosed). All policy payments that have been made be reimbursed to the estate of the subject and should there be any claim on the policy, it should be denied based on the contestability and suicide clause. I.e. Mental Illness at the initiation of coverage and the demise of the insurer by her own hand.

Signed: MacArthur O'Rourke, Senior Investigator 15 December 1991.

Science Says Eat Dark Chocolate for Health Benefits
By Toni Denis

POPULAR FILMS PORTRAY CHOCOLATE as an aphrodisiac, as in the novels "Like Water for Chocolate" by Laura Esquivel, and "Chocolat." by Joanne Harris. In those two novels turned movies, the main characters seduce or are seduced by hot chocolate and a chocolatier's wares. While there is a scientific basis for the feeling of well-being quality cocoa and dark chocolate produces, recently studies also show that dark chocolate has an array of other health benefits when eaten in moderation.

The health benefits of chocolate have been touted since the days of Montezuma, the Aztec chief, who drank up to 50 cups of a cocoa concoction daily to give himself special powers. Considered the "food of the gods," the mostly bitter drink derived from fermented cacao seeds and flavored with cinnamon and herbs, was called "Xocoatl." Later, Spanish monks who settled in the New World derived the word "chocolate" from the Aztec word, and made it the drink more palatable by adding sugar.

In the many years since chocolate became a global taste sensation, scientific studies begun in the mid-'90s by the chocolate company MARS found that the cocoa butter in dark chocolate contains heart-healthy mono-unsaturated fatty acid, or MUFA, which is similar to olive oil. The MARS Center for Cocoa Health Science, formally established in 2012, as done extensive studies on how MUFA allows unsaturated fats easily glide through the bloodstream and help unclog and protect arteries from building up. Chocolate must contain at least 70% cocoa content to have this benefit—the definition of dark chocolate.

Dark Chocolate Is Heart Healthy

In recent years, a deluge of independently verified studies by international researchers have confirmed the MARS studies, such as a report in the British Medical Journal that found that eating dark chocolate could reduce the risk of developing heart disease by one-third. Also, the Journal of Nutrition found that plant sterols and cocoa flavanols are proven to reduce bad cholesterol and high blood pressure. Other reported benefits include:

Prevents Stroke

In a study of 44,489 people, Canadian researchers found that those who consumed dark chocolate regularly were 22% less likely to have a stroke than those who did not. Of those who had a stroke and consumed chocolate, they were 46% less likely to die as a result.

Reduces Appetite

Other studies have found that the MUFAs in dark chocolate help reduce appetite. This helps combat cortisol, a hormone that causes stress eating and induces cravings for sugar and fat.

Positively affects Insulin

Dark chocolate helps control insulin levels and relax blood vessels, lowering blood pressure.

Provides Minerals

There's a reason why women, especially, may crave chocolate. One dark chocolate square naturally provides important minerals, including magnesium, copper, calcium and iron. Women tend to need more calcium and iron than men in their diets.

Reduces Inflammation and Helps Peripheral Artery Disease Patients

Flavanols, a kind of antioxidant in dark chocolate, boosts good HDL cholesterol and reduces bad LDL levels, reducing inflammation. Flavanols are plant pigments found in dark green vegetables, berries, green tea, nuts, spices, red wine and chocolate. Antioxidants help the body's cells resist damage caused by free radicals. It's the anti-inflammatory qualities that offer protection against cancer, heart disease and type 2 diabetes. In addition, a study by the Journal of the American Heart Association found that Peripheral Artery Disease patients who consumed dark chocolate were able to walk farther, due to its artery opening qualities.

These benefits are not available in most milk chocolate, however. All chocolate starts out as dark chocolate, but when dairy is added it becomes milk chocolate. Dairy products, unfortunately, negate many health benefits of dark chocolate by reducing cocoa content in favor of adding unhealthy fats and a load of sugar.

Mass produced milk chocolate is derived from Belgian bulk chocolate, which is sold to many American chocolate makers. There are lots of problems with this chocolate from an ethical standpoint—often the cacao is picked and processed through child labor in West Africa. In addition, the cacao farmers are not paid a fair price for the product they sell. If they were, it would be called Fair Trade chocolate. Once this chocolate is sold in bulk, heavy processing and additives, flavorings, sometimes caffeine and a majority of sugar make it far less desirable. The first and main ingredient listed on most milk chocolate packages is usually sugar.

The healthiest chocolate is organic, Fair Trade dark chocolate. It comes from Central and South America but can also originate from such far-flung locales as Tanzania, Madagascar, Viet Nam and other tropical locations where cacao seeds grow.

Buying quality Fair Trade dark chocolate not only ensures that it's quality chocolate, but also can make buyers feel good about eating something that benefits many otherwise struggling farmers around the world—a psychological benefit that doesn't need a scientific study to prove. Many of these chocolate bars can be found in high-end grocery stores and health food stores.

Happy Birthday, William Shakespeare
By Steve Healey

KNOCK, KNOCK. WHO'S THERE? Why it's William Shakespeare. And *as good luck would have it,* today is his birthday! As a master of the **Queen's English**, Shakespeare determined that *all the world's a stage and the men and women are merely players*. Though many people walk around saying, "I never could understand Shakespeare. It *was Greek to me,*" his work is timeless. To them I say, *"Mum's the word."* They *doth protest too much, methinks*.

I know my writing can't *hold a candle* to anything he wrote and *there's the rub*. How could I possibly come up with a way to honor him and take *cold comfort* in the fact that I will not become a *laughing stock* and make my friends declare, *"Off with his head!"*

The naked truth is that we writers, in our minds, sometimes believe *we few, we happy few, we band of brothers* and sisters are *the be-all and end-all* of the future of writing. That we are the indication of a *sea change* in the way literature will be written. That in *one fell swoop*, we will be the new Shakespeare. *The fatal vision* in this is that most of us refuse to realize that eventually, unlike Shakespeare, our works *will vanish into thin air.*

The long and the short of it is that a William Shakespeare only comes along every couple hundred years. And this simple fact puts us writers *in a pickle*.

We love our writing, but *our love is blind*. No matter how much we *night owls* burn the midnight oil, in the light of *the working day world,* the *daily bag and baggage* of life, we are required to be a responsible *tower of strength* while we wish to be *fancy free* and do nothing but write to our *heart's content*. There is no real *rhyme nor reason* to expect life to *budge an inch* and let us *play fast and loose* with *such stuff that dreams are made on*.

So, *woe is me*. Maybe it's *a wild goose chase* that I'm on, that my possibility of becoming a famous writer has *seen better days*. Maybe I *should be up in arms* about the way life has shown me nothing but *foul play* in this.

However, I will not continue to *wear my heart on my sleeve* and let Life *throw cold water* on *the method in my madness*. I will continue to *cry "Havoc" and let loose the dogs of war* on the literary world. I will not accept that **what's done is done** and will continue to write just as though **the world's mine oyster.**

For now though, I must say farewell. **Parting is such sweet sorrow,** but this little creation has become **too much of a good thing.** It's **high time** to end this piece. However take comfort in the fact that **all's well that ends well.**

So, to **come full circle**, I say once again, Happy Birthday to William Shakespeare, someone who really knew how to express **what a piece of work is a man.**

When you focus on someone's disability you'll overlook their abilities, beauty and uniqueness. Once you learn to accept and love them for who they are, you subconsciously learn to love yourself unconditionally.
—*Yvonne Pierre*

Tickets
By Shirley Willis

UP FROM WHERE I LIVE, Orion makes high siren sounds like an ambulance or a cop car. He also wears a too-big black hat like the bad guy in an old Western. I walk, and he weaves in and out of cars. Weaves between me and the other kids on bikes. He's all pointy sharpness and sinuous plasticity that spurt simultaneously from his compact self like cactus and orchids. Everyone honks and waves at him.

He tracks me, tells me how to be safe. "Don't go so fast." "Face the traffic." "Stay outta the road." He figure-eights' ahead and back. Rears his bike in front of me like a stallion. Pushes his hat back from his eyes. Spits off to the side like the big boys. Hands me a yellow stickie scrawled with, "Tikt for sped. 35 in 25 mi zun."

His numbers and letters are backward. Or upside down.

I put the "ticket" in my pocket, "Sorry, Officer. Won't happen again." Then maneuver past.

He follows, races ahead, circles back, tires slewing small rocks. "That stump? You know the one you took? My dad dug that outta our back yard."

I keep walking. Orion sizes me up, western style, hat askew.

"Bet you didn't know that when you took it," he yells. "Didn't know my dad dug it out."

For weeks, the stump reclined with disassembled seduction. Stripped branch-bare. In different lights, it was the Matisse Blue Nude, a muted Picasso I can't quite remember or, maybe the Ingres Odalisque. Distant. Compelling. All that. Begging to be staged. But not against the water tank in the no man's land at the end of the road.

I had to have it.

The boy points a gun finger. "Well. I saw that stump on your yard. Down the hill where you live."

I keep walking. "You need it back?"

"It's okay you took it." He follows along. "But it's really my dad's."

We move along the road together, him peddling, me stepping.

"Well, here's the deal," I say.

He slows. "Yeah?"

"Any time you want that stump back? Anytime. You come on down and get it."

"Owl."

"What?"

"My head hurts. Sometimes. Like, really owl!" He means "Ow."

"Now?"

"Yeah. They took that little piece outta my head." He rides his bike with no hands, pinches his forefinger and thumb to show me. "Little. Like this."

I slide my arm toward my left boob.

Cancer. His brain and my boob. He doesn't know it but we both paid the same ticket to keep on driving.

We move together toward the end of the road.

Traffic thins. From an open door, his gramma yells him to dinner.

His dad stands by the pickup in the driveway and waves. "Listen to your gramma. You hear now?" A world of sweet and sad drawls through his words.

The boy stops by his driveway. Shouts after me. "That ticket? It's just a warning."

Expository Essay

The American Rattlesnake
By Pat Fogarty

Yogi Berra, a man noted for his sagacious quips, once said, "There are some people, who if they don't already know, you can't tell them." Yogi's tidbit of worldly advice is especially true when it comes to rattlesnakes.

The rattlesnake is the most feared animal in the western hemisphere. The distinctive sound made by the rattle of its tail is an eloquent warning that few misinterpret.

Most sane people, who come across a rattlesnake have the genetically inherited common sense to cease all forward motion and back away from the creature. Unfortunately, every year approximately seven thousand people receive a venomous bite from this cold-blooded carnivorous reptile. And interestingly, it should not surprise the intelligent reader that seventy percent of the people bit by a rattlesnake are males between the ages of sixteen and twenty-seven. Most of us know the type—they are the self-imagined invincible ones who believe they know it all. It's usually not a good practice to cast blame on a dimwitted victim. But let's be honest; being a show-off and messing with a rattlesnake is just plain dumb.

The powerful hollow fangs of the rattlesnake can pierce the thick hide of a buffalo. They function like natural hypodermic needles and are capable of injecting a lethal dose of poison when the snake senses a threat.

Toxic compounds in the venom destroy tissue and kill blood cells. This wreaks havoc with the circulatory system. It also causes internal bleeding and respiratory failure. Besides the acute pain from the toxins, survivors often lose fingers, toes, feet, and hands. So, even if you are wearing gloves and high leather boots, you should give a rattlesnake a wide berth if you ever encounter one.

Native American cultures held conflicting opinions of the rattlesnake. Some pre-Columbian tribes considered the snake to be a good omen because of its power to kill. And, other tribes perceived the snake's ability to kill as a sign of evil and destruction. But, regardless of how a tribe viewed the creature—the rattlesnake was an important part of their culture. Totems of the serpent were used in their sacred rituals. And, the canyons of the arid American southwest are riddled with prehistoric rock art depicting the rattlesnake and other indigenous animals.

On the other side of the North American continent, in the State of Ohio, hundreds of earthen mounds built by Native Americans dot the landscape. Many are over three thousand years old. The most striking mound created by Native Americans is in the shape of a snake. Stretching more than 400 meters "Serpent Mound" is the largest surviving example of a prehistoric effigy mound in the world. The beautifully preserved ancient earthwork depicts the form of a slithering serpent with an oval shaped head.

In Mesoamerica, an area we now call Central America, the Aztec civilization worshiped a Plumed Serpent they named Quetzalcoatl—a god that took the combined form of a bird and rattlesnake. Throughout Central and South America images of the snake are a common find at archeological sites.

In modern times, the habitat of this venomous pit viper extends from the mountains of southwestern Canada, to the grassy plains of northern Argentina.

There are thirty-six known species of rattlesnakes with about seventy subspecies. Make no mistake, they are all dangerous. But, by far the deadliest rattlesnake in the world is the Mohave rattlesnake. In its natural desert environment; camouflage, speed, and aggressiveness enhance its ability to kill small rodents and birds. However, those attributes in the viper increases the danger of a hiker or camper being bit. The snake is greenish brown in color, and when fully grown it's about thirty inches long. But, don't let its size deceive you. The venom of the Mohave rattlesnake is conservatively estimated to be ten times more lethal than any other rattlesnake. So obviously, if you are hiking in an area where these creatures reside; be extremely careful where you step. Very few people survive a nip in the leg from this serpent.

A few years ago, an Arizona woman living in the small town of Paulden was bit by a Mohave rattlesnake when she stepped out of her home to walk to her car. The neurotoxins in a Mohave's venom are very deceiving and the bite did not seem serious to her. The woman's first instinct was to strike back at the snake. She picked up a garden rake and unknowingly wasted precious time trying to kill the elusive reptile. Within minutes she was writhing in pain and gasping for air. Her husband rushed from the house, realized what had happened and called for an ambulance. The emergency dispatcher understood the seriousness of the situation and sent a helicopter to airlift the woman to a hospital in Flagstaff. She died on the way.

So, if you happen to hear the unique sound made by the flickering of a rattlesnake's tail—stop moving, try to assess the location of the snake, and by all means retreat.

However, if you ever visit the Catalina Isles, beware of the oxymoronic Catalina rattlesnake. Over the centuries the rattlesnakes on the Catalina Isles in the Gulf of California have evolved, and these deadly creatures no longer have the ability to grow a rattle.

The Spelling Test
By Sue Favia

BY THE THIRD GRADE, I was getting to know the reputations and unique characteristics of some the nuns at St. Katharine's Elementary School, at least at the lower grade levels, which was the entire first floor. Sister Norton stood out among them all as the most feared. After only two years of schooling, my reputation seemed to precede me as well. I was the third Favia, following my two older sisters.

After our combined six years of delinquent tuition and book bills, the nuns were not happy to see one more Favia on their roster who couldn't pay her way. So, I was marked before I even walked through the door.

The nuns were on a short fuse most of the time, and any spark could set them off. It seemed that I short-circuited them more than most, and Sister Norton was one of the worst nuns for impulsive, unpredictable, and very strange behaviors. She would roll up taffy into little bite-sized balls and keep them in her top desk drawer. Eating was not allowed in the classroom, other than lunch, and our candy break. Despite this, Sister Norton would sometimes slip a piece of taffy into her mouth when she thought no one was looking. But I was looking. She must have rolled them each morning before class.

One morning, after a particularly violent disciplinary confrontation, she tried to bribe me with one of her taffy balls. It disgusted me as she cautiously leaned over my desk, nudged one into my hand, and whispered,

"Susan, your mother doesn't need to know about this morning." I put my hand up to my mouth, mimicking a chewing motion as I pretended to eat it. As if her sweaty, smelly taffy ball was a fair exchange for my secrecy. I never talked to anyone about the abuses anyway. Not even to my friends who were present in class, the ones who saw the terror on my face and the tears in my eyes as I stood in the middle of seventy classmates. I wanted to be someone else with my friends. I didn't want to be the person they saw being belittled and humiliated.

It was late afternoon, and our class was taking a candy break after lunch. It was one of those rare occasions where I joined in the line of the candy privileged. But I knew how to save money when I wanted to. When I found a penny, I'd put it away until I found another penny, or I'd find a pop bottle to exchange for two pennies. I had a keen eye and a good ear for copper hitting pavement, and I could see the reflection of a pop bottle a block away. And on the home front, the back of the couch, after my father was done with his nap, was where treasures were found.

I knew what I wanted well before I got to the front of the line—the biggest chocolate bar there was. I paid my five cents and took it to my desk as if it were a badge of honor, making a point not to rip it open too quickly. Savoring the pleasure, I propped it up on the front of my desk, letting it sit for a few minutes, proud of my constraint. I also wanted my classmates to see that I could afford to buy candy, too.

We had a fifteen-minute bathroom or candy break, or both if we were fast enough. The class was still silently walking back and forth, each row of students taking their turn in the hall to purchase their sweets, on the long fold-up table, when Linda Musgrave tapped me on my shoulder.

"I'll trade your candy bar for my Cinderella wallet," she said.

Huh, was she crazy? A Cinderella wallet for a candy bar? I'd have traded my shoes for that.

Okay," I said, tempering my excitement. I was exploding inside at the prospect of owning a Cinderella wallet. Other than a Cinderella watch, nothing could have surpassed this exchange, and Linda Musgrave was offering me this treasure for one Snickers bar.

I barely took a breath before grabbing the candy bar off my desk and agreeing to the swap. I held on firmly to the bar as I handed it back to her, holding out my other hand for the wallet. When I was certain I had a secure grip on the wallet, I let go of my candy. I flipped around in my seat, gazing at my new wallet for a moment, touching and tracing Cinderella with my fingers before opening it to inspect all the features inside. The wallet was pale blue, with a white inlaid center and Cinderella wearing her blue and white dress, with her golden-yellow hair pulled high on her head, tied with a blue ribbon. Inside were clear plastic inserts for photos with another slot for my identification. My name. I couldn't wait to see it in my best cursive writing. On the other side of the wallet was a little pouch for change, with a flap to keep my money from falling out and a strap that snapped the wallet closed for safety.

While I was examining the photo insert, it slipped out of the slot. It seemed like a simple thing to fix, but I fumbled for a while and couldn't put it back in its place. I was becoming frustrated and certain that I'd broken the wallet before I even got to show it off. Linda had already consumed the entire candy bar and was licking the melted chocolate off her thumb when I turned around and told her I thought I broke it. I asked her how to put the photo insert back in place.

"Oh sure, that's easy. Let me show you," she said, and I handed it back to her. I was thrilled to see how quickly she replaced the tab, relieved that I hadn't broken it. As I reached back to retrieve my wallet, she pulled her hand away to keep it out of my reach.

"What are you doing? Give it back!" I demanded, reaching over her desk and trying to grab her arm. Our desks were catty-corner to each other and butted up together, as was every other row to allow more space in the room. This arrangement made it easier for us to talk and reach back and forth.

"I changed my mind," she snapped, pushing my arm away. Now she slid the wallet into her desk. I couldn't believe what was happening.

"That's my wallet! We made a deal, and you ate my candy bar. Now give it back to me." Now my squeal caught Sister Norton's attention.

"What's going on over there, Miss Favia?" she said with her usual irritation when she spoke to me.

"Linda took my wallet, s'ter, and won't give it back to me," I said.

"Do you have her wallet, Miss Musgrave?"

"No, Sister, I only let her see it, and then she tried taking it from me. It's mine, Sister. My mother bought it for me last week," Linda replied with a smirk

"That's a lie, sister, I traded it for my Snickers bar and she ate th—"

"Turn around, Miss Favia," she said, discounting my response and cutting me off. "Class get your paper out for your spelling test."

The conversation was over. I knew not to persist. Arguing with Sister Norton would prove to be far worse than losing a wallet. I was crushed by the loss of what had almost been mine, even if for just a moment. I felt cheated and betrayed, and I was angry that I let it happen.

Linda and I had never been friends, though we weren't really enemies either. We just never played together, and we never walked to or from school together, even though we only lived a few blocks away. If we were ten feet from one another on the same sidewalk, we would have stayed that way all the way to school. She had a way of looking at me that let me know she wasn't interested in being friends. Linda was the tomboy type and had a tough nature about her. She never actually did anything to me, but I always had a sense that at the slightest provocation, she could—and would. She was much taller and heavier than I, so, there was no way I could intimidate or force her to return the wallet after school.

Gone were my nickel, my candy bar, and my Cinderella wallet. I tried to hold back my tears and anger as I prepared for our spelling test. Everything had to be taken off our desks, so we were not tempted to cheat and look at our books. We had to spell twenty words that were taken directly from our spelling workbook, and Sister Norton always recited them in the exact same order as the text. But for extra precaution, Sister Norton had spelling guards that walked up and down each aisle, watching to see that no one peeked into their desks to look at the words or try any other methods of cheating.

We had those old wooden oak desks with black scrolled wrought iron frames and legs. We could slide our books and papers in and out of the opening, making easy access for slipping the workbook out of the desk just enough to peek at the words as the spelling guard moved down the aisle. Sister Norton always chose the smart students as spelling guards during the test because she knew they could spell any word that was in the book. The smart ones were always chosen to help the nuns: washing the blackboards, distributing worksheets, handing out tests, passing out holy cards for outstanding work, or guarding the bathrooms to see that there was no talking there either. Next up in rank to the spelling guards were the patrol boys, and only second in line of importance to the altar boys, who were supreme among them all.

Before and after school, the patrol boys stood between the two single-file lines with their white straps around their waists and crossed diagonally over their chests. Their job was to make sure no one talked or stepped out of place. It must have been that diagonal strap that made them feel like little soldiers or maybe cadets. Our lines formed at the threshold of the classroom door, threading through the long hallway, down the stairs to the main floor, and out of the school grounds for an entire block before we could fall out of line, and silence.

Sister Norton began reciting the spelling words one at a time, allowing a moment before moving on to the next word. At every opportunity after each word, I turned around to give Linda another look of contempt and disapproval in hope that she would change her mind and offer the wallet back to me. Her head didn't budge as she hovered over her paper. Again, after the next spelling word, I tried to get her attention, hoping to find a shred of remorse or shame. But her physical demeanor didn't change, and she never diverted her eyes from her paper. She held her head low, letting her straight sandy-brown hair hang over her paper as if she were afraid someone might copy her spelling words.

As the next word was recited, I looked back again and caught sight of something very strange. I waited for the next word to be called, and then more carefully turned around to be certain of my observation. What I saw was the slightest offset of a second piece of paper, carefully placed underneath Linda's spelling sheet. On my next glance, I knew she had written the entire twenty words on the second sheet. While spelling each word on her test paper, she had the bottom sheet with the correct words already written. Linda would then, I surmised, slip the top sheet back into her desk when the test was over, leaving the correctly spelled words ready to hand in.

Now, had I been smart—and I wasn't—I would have blackmailed her into giving me the wallet back. But, I didn't realize that I had leverage, so instead, I did what any scorned eight-year-old girl would do. Rat on her! Squeal! Sing like a canary! I doubt Linda even realized that I saw what she was doing before I raised my hand to even the score. It was a rare occasion that I raised my hand for anything, other than to go to the lavatory, so when my arm went up, particularly during a test, Sister Norton seemed surprised—or was it annoyance?

"Yes, Susan—what is it?"

"Sister, Linda Musgrave is cheating on her spelling test," I said with the triumph of the victor.

You could almost feel the air sucked from the room as everyone simultaneously gasped and inhaled. All that was left was a frightening silence as the spelling guard swiftly moved in on his prey and stood at her side like a proud centurion waiting for Sister Norton to take action. Then, that terrifying and oh-so-familiar swooshing of her habit and the clicking of her beads as she entered the narrow aisle with a swift stride. Only this time she wasn't coming after me. You could feel the pounding of her feet on the wooden floor as everyone sat motionless in their own self-preservation. Now I knew what it was like being on the "other side;" they were scared too. As Sister Norton reached Linda's desk, she grabbed her spelling papers in a rage. Seeing what Linda had done, she crumpled them up in her pasty white fist.

"Stand up, Miss Musgrave—stand up!" she screamed.

Now, Linda was in group two, which was the average-level students. I don't remember her ever getting into trouble. I assumed she would have to stay after class for at least a week, not be allowed to go outside for recess after lunch and would very likely have to write on the blackboard a hundred times one of the Ten Commandments that best represented her offense. That's usually what happened to the 'good kids' gone bad. It all happened so fast...

"Open your mouth," Sister Norton shouted. Linda had a confused look on her face, as did I and the rest of the class.

"Did you hear what I said? Open your mouth!" Linda parted her lips slightly as if to speak, and the next thing I saw was Sister Norton stuffing the wad of papers into Linda's mouth, forcing it open wider—the entire spelling test.

"Open, I said!" she screamed over and over, stuffing and twisting, making sure it wouldn't fall out. There Linda stood, tears streaming down her face and her mouth wide open, stuffed with her spelling test—both sheets. And in the next moment, Sister Norton spun around and rattled and swooshed back to her desk, continuing with the next spelling word as if nothing had happened. Linda stood in unimaginable humiliation next to her desk, crying and drooling through the wads of paper.

Oh no, what have I done? I felt my face go hot and my heart beat at an alarming speed while I struggled to complete my test, never turning my head or even my eyes in Linda's direction.

The rest of the day was a blur. I couldn't concentrate on anything. My mind was racing, and I couldn't formulate a full thought. This was not what was supposed to happen. I only remember thinking; *How will I get home?* I never had the foresight to consider what the consequences could be, for either one of us.

My short life flashed before me. I envisioned Linda's chubby fist traveling toward my face as she sat on top of me just out of the vision of the patrol boys—or worse, me running for my life every day after school, wondering when and where she would catch up with me and wreak her revenge. I was already strategizing on how I would get home, how many yards or alleys I could cut through before she would spring on me. I was counting on Norton keeping her after class, at least the first day. That was the normal procedure after any violation of rules. But this was by no means a normal day, and Linda left school, as usual, in front of me in line.

As the line split up a block away from school, I slowed down and pulled back as far as possible, walking as close to other kids as I could. I knew she wouldn't hurt me if I was in a crowd. But one by one, with each passing block, the kids thinned out. And then I was walking alone, holding back almost a full block behind Linda, darting behind parked cars and bushes until she turned two blocks before my house. I was safe for now, but then there was going a tomorrow and a tomorrow for the rest of my school days.

This routine went on for weeks; I would walk a block behind Linda and then duck off into a backyard to take another way home. My wandering nature certainly paid off. I must have known a dozen or more ways of getting home: across prairies and fields, over fences, and through backyards and alleys.

Linda must have been so traumatized that she was afraid to even look at me, much less speak to me or treat me badly. But I still kept my distance from her, never losing sight of that day and always wondering when she would snap and retaliate. As the months passed, I became less cautious, and the space between us grew shorter, but never too close to inflame an old wound. And for the next five years at St. Katharine's School, we never spoke another word, nor any time thereafter.

Truth is so rare that it is delightful to tell it.
—Emily Dickinson

Nobody
By Bruce D. Sparks

GROWING UP IN A SMALL TOWN, I wanted to be a lot of things. A happy man never really was part of those dreams. I thought as long as you were something, happiness would be yours. Being something or nothing was all I thought about. Something would be what everybody else was, and nothing would be what nobody was. The more time I spent on the subject the more I realized I wanted to be a nobody. Nobody could do anything he wanted to 'cause he wasn't locked into being somebody like everyone else. Once I had my mind made up, I started off to become a nobody.

The first step to being a nobody was to become a paperboy. Nobody knows their paperboy. He is just the nobody that delivers the newspapers they read—so they can be somebody. He never reads them 'cause that would tend to make him a somebody. Even when he comes to your house to collect the paper bill, he is still a nobody. Yuma Daily Sun for 75 cents a week or $2 a month--not a bad deal to learn all you need to know to be somebody. Mary Ann Palmer didn't know who I was when I came to her house to collect. She was somebody to me and I noticed her right away, even at my young age. Absolutely gorgeous, and she was always nice to me. I thought we had a connection once upon a time. Guess I was daydreaming 'cause it turns out I was nobody to her.

I came up with an idea to buy a crystal radio set and listen to late-night radio out of Texas or Oklahoma. So, I got me one and put it together. Each night I would tune in to some show on the airwaves and listen to the music of the day through the earpiece. I really thought I was a nobody then 'cause nobody listened to the radio in the middle of the night.

One night I went outside with my radio to try to get better reception and found it was 10 times better out there. Mom got mad at me for being up past bedtime and for listening to God knows what on that radio. She took it away from me saying, "You must think you're somebody to do that sort of thing." She got me to wondering if maybe I was turning into a somebody.

Used to borrow my dad's .22 rifle and go out shooting on the desert.

Long as I kept the rifle clean for my dad to use, I could use it anytime I wanted. In Yuma, summer days would get well over 100 degrees, but I didn't mind a bit. I'd go out on the desert a mile or two from the house and hunt snakes and rabbits. I figured I must be a nobody 'cause nobody goes out on the desert in Yuma in the middle of the day.

Always had a natural eye, as my dad would say, to shoot things dead center every time. Never feared getting bit by a snake 'cause I could see for miles in all directions at once, so it seemed. Nobody could do that.

I told my brother that I could shoot really good and I always hit the snakes in the head.

He said, "That's because the snake has such keen eyesight he can look right down the barrel of the gun when you point it at him and see the bullet coming. Snakes are so fast they actually strike at the bullet as it nears 'em."

So even if I was a bad shot, I would get my fair share of head shots, too. He was my older brother and stood there lying to me as big as you please. I guess he thought I was a nobody and it didn't matter if he lied to me. I didn't care 'cause I was truly becoming a nobody.

With two older brothers, my clothes were hand-me-downs all my life and already somewhat threadbare. Just the clothes a nobody like me would wear, but always clean from the homemade lye soap that Mom used to wash our clothes. My dad believed that boys didn't need hair while growing up. "High and tight" was his motto and he owned the clippers in our house. So, I was a real nobody in clean, ironed, faded-out clothes and no hair.

Took on the task of working for extra spending money by cleaning up back yards and throwing out trash for people. While cleaning up the back yard of old Mr. Webster, a man that went to our church, I found something of interest. It was wrapped in burlap bags and wired up tight like a mummy, as if it could get away if not treated in such a manner. When I asked about it, he said it was of no importance to him and that I should just throw it out with the other unwanted junk from bygone years. Like any boy my age, I had to know what it was, and what I found when I unwrapped it was breathtaking. It was a 1946 Matchless 750cc one-cylinder motorcycle with the chain missing, and no wheels or tires. It was beautiful, like nothing I had ever seen before. It had a little brass plaque stuck on the gas tank that read: "Track Record - Salinas, California - 1950-1951 - 98 MPH."

I asked if I could have the motorcycle since he was going to throw it out anyway. He looked at me like I was crazy. "Boy, this is the machine that took my brother from me. Hell, this machine is a killer and it sure isn't for children to be playing with even if it will never run again. Just you throw it out and forget about it." I told him I would take it in pay for my work, and I would even clean out his shed and straighten up everything for it. He looked at me for a long time, then at the motorcycle.

"I know of two other people that died riding that God-forsaken machine. As sure as I'm standing here, it will kill you, too. But if you think you can get it started and ride it without going to meet your Maker, you're welcome to it. Just swear you will never try racing it." I swore that I wouldn't, and I really thought I had the better end of this bargain. Nobody had one of these, I thought, and away I went dragging it home, much to my dad's dismay.

I tried real hard to get it running. Engine came apart easily enough and I could tell even with my limited ability that the rings were shot, so I could get no compression when trying to start it. Dad, being an auto mechanic, looked it over and decided DeSoto rings of that size would work. So, I bought a set and put the engine back together with a new gasket here, and new tapped and threaded bolt there, hoping it would start, but secretly praying it wouldn't. I did not want any part of going 90-plus miles an hour on this old beast with very little in the way of brakes. But then brakes wouldn't make it run. One thing at a time, I thought, and put brakes at the end of my fix-it list.

I figured that a somebody wouldn't even try to fix this old relic, but a nobody like me was perfect for the job. Cleaned out and reset the carburetor. Adjusted the old magneto, drained and refilled the crank case and transmission. Then came the clutch—all I could do was clean it, sand it a bit, and hope it would work. Then with everything ready I gave her a stomp with the old kicker. I remember yelling as the beast roared to life, "Holy Sh—!"

Run it did and very well for an old hunk of metal that had been in captivity for some 15-odd years. I could tell I had a handful with this machine. Time after time it fired right up and ran like it was brand new and breathing fresh air for the first time after being bound and gagged all those years. Now all I really needed were tires, wheels, and a chain to make her go. I also needed brakes to make her stop, but that was still at the bottom of my list.

My dad, having been a motorcycle rider in his youth, was just as interested in getting the thing going as I was. Took a while but soon the bike was together and ready to ride. I had Harley Davidson wheels and tires, a new chain and drive sprockets. Dad was taking no chances and took me out to the desert on the hardpack to ride the machine, away from everyone and everything. Said if I killed myself he would bury me right there on the spot and bring Mom by on my birthday to visit. Fitting for a nobody, I thought, and it just might happen.

I had no choice in the matter, you know. Men, and boys, too, sometimes put themselves into situations like this without thinking. It's a macho thing we do, the rite of passage to manhood. I wanted to be a man even if a nobody type of man. So, with an old army helmet I had found and a beat-up pair of welding goggles, I fired up the machine and sat on it while it warmed up. A slight adjustment to the fuel mixture and I was ready to ride. With clutch in I stomped it into first gear and got ready to go. I looked at my dad with one last look. You might know the look I'm talking about. The look that says, "I don't really want to do this, but if you're not going to stop me then I'll have to do it." He didn't do or say a thing, and the silence from him was almost louder than the motorcycle.

I still remember that feeling as the bike took off and I was hanging on with every bit of strength I could muster. The hand throttle went to full open and stuck in that position, which was something I had not counted on. Here is where I mention two points about speed. One is fast and can take some time to achieve. The other is quick, which takes no time at all to achieve. I had never been to 90-plus miles per hour in my short life, not ever, and certainly not as quick as that machine between my shaky legs was taking me there.

We were absolutely flying, and I was on my way to the ride of a lifetime for sure. Having bought my ticket to ride, I was going to stick it out. I swear death was approaching me as fast as I was approaching the horizon. That little brass plaque kept running through my mind about the 98 miles per hour record in Salinas, California, the three dead riders that went before me, and the everlasting reminder of how brakes should not be last on anyone's list of needed parts. The brakes didn't work, and the clutch would not disengage. The increase in speed was happening faster than I could handle, and even with goggles firmly in place I was losing my ability to focus.

Then I had a brainstorm. I reached down and pulled the fuel line from the gas tank and held the clutch in for all I was worth. I swear it took what seemed like a lifetime, but it died for lack of fuel and finally came to a stop, after covering the other half of Yuma County.

I got off of that silent machine, laid it down none too gingerly, walked several steps and collapsed on the ground near it, but not so close that it could touch me. Dad drove up in the truck to where I was. It took him a while—I must have covered five miles. He said, "Damn, Boy, that thing is a rocket." I looked at him and said, "I want to go home." We loaded up the bike in the truck and drove back home. Dad never said a word all the way there. I didn't mind; I had some thinking to do. I needed to evaluate my decision to be a nobody.

Dad adjusted the throttle, so it would work right, and fixed the fuel line and brakes. He rode the bike several times around the block and back and forth to work and told me the bike ran just fine. That was as close to dying as I had come in my young life. I saw the face of death and had lived to tell the tale. I knew that if I ever rode that machine again, it was going to kill me. I looked at it many times after that, but I never did ride it again.

I recounted the event to the man who gave me the machine, and he went into the story of how it had killed this guy, and mangled that guy, and so on. Said that motorcycle was the cause of at least three deaths that he knew of. He looked me straight in the eye and said, "Son, you are a very lucky boy." I knew for certain that death could be cheated. There would be other times in years to come.

I have had other motorcycles in my life and I was a motorcycle policeman for a number of years. Riding motorcycles for pay was easy and challenging with the right training. Riding them for fun and pleasure is exciting if you know what you are doing. Riding a motorcycle because you want to prove you are a man, or a nobody for that matter, is stupid and childish, especially if you have never done it before. My dad knew that, but it was something I had to learn on my own. Some things in life are like that.

That old motorcycle and the ride it gave me changed my thinking. To be somebody wasn't a bad thing, and happiness can be yours if you put in the effort required. To be a nobody takes a lot of work and most of it amounts to nothing. I decided I was just too lazy for that. At 14 years old I figured out something that I had been working on for some time. I was getting to know the person I was becoming. I even had thoughts of doing something great with the time I had left to live, and it felt pretty good. Hell, I might even turn out to be somebody--that is, if I can live long enough.

The Leader of the Band
By John Maher

ENERGIZED AND FIT, I trudged up "Heartbreak Hill #1" on my daily 3½-mile morning trek around Prescott Canyon Estates. I had The Rolling Stones on my iPod, the sun strong, the sky cloudless and brilliant Arizona blue, the air crisp and cool. All was right in my world.

My daily walks include a regular internal dialog. Random thoughts breeze into my consciousness, and I kick them around until another surfaces. I enjoyed listening to my music and quiet reflection, my style of meditation. Sometimes a song will trigger a long-buried memory, a tender reminiscence. And I give myself to contemplating

On this day, as I strode along breathing in the bracing air, I examined the productive actions I was taking for my health, steps I hadn't adhered to when I was working full-time. After retiring eight years ago, I put being healthy at the top of my to-do list. I work out daily, starting with my jaunt around the hillsides where I live. I stretch, I lift weights, I do cardio exercises.

As I was reviewing this litany of steps and giving myself a high five, I said, "I know I'm gonna die, just not any time soon" … and the instant this thought occurred, I realized it was a favorite maxim of The Old Man. My next thoughts flashed to that hospital room in San Jose, California on that dismal day in early November 1990.

Tom, my older brother and the family's designated administrator-in-chief, called me at my job in New York City with the news. "The Old Man's cancer's back. He's in the hospital. It's inoperable. They're discharging him Saturday. You'd better come out." Unsaid but understood, The Old Man was terminal, and they were shipping him home to die. I needed to fly to California to say my goodbyes. Two days later, I was on an American Airlines non-stop from New York to San Jose.

Tom and my younger brother Patrick met me at the San Jose airport. When the three of us got together, laughter and comedy ensued, leading to total bedlam. Because both brothers lived in Los Angeles and I lived in

New York, our get-togethers were annual events. The airport welcoming's tended to be even more raucous from pent-up anticipation. This time it was small hellos, brief hugs, and limited conversation. The ride to the hospital was quiet and solemn.

When we turned and got off the elevator on the third floor of the hospital, I peered down the short bright cream-painted corridor into my father's dimly lit room. He was sitting in profile on the edge of his lowered hospital bed. His elbows were on his knees, his head hung over, the silhouette of the beaten contender on his stool in the corner.

I came in the door first and rested my palm on The Old Man's shoulder in greeting. It was bone, no muscle. I was stunned. My father was always well-built, muscular, 190 pounds, with deltoid shoulders like small boulders. A gifted natural athlete with God-given talent, as a young man he earned money as a pro football player and as a light heavyweight prizefighter. When he retired from the book publishing business in his late sixties, he bought a condo next to a golf course. He played 18 holes every day, Monday through Friday and 36 holes on Saturday and Sunday. Vanity kept him doing his Canadian Air Force exercise routine every morning until cancer lodged in his colon at age 78. Now he was that detested object, a veritable bag of bones. I felt heartsick.

I gritted my teeth and said, "Hey Pop."

He swung his head and peered at me, his ice-blue eyes glazed and used up, the fire gone. He replied in a labored voice, "Hey John-o." He noticed my hand lingering on his bony shoulder as if waiting for a miraculous change, and he said with faint recognition, "No meat left there."

"Ah, what the hell, Pop," I said. I pulled up a chair and mimicked his elbows-on-knees posture. Tom and Patrick came in the room, murmured hellos, and stood behind me their arms folded in anticipation. We tried to exchange banal pleasantries… how was your flight, how are the kids, how's your job… but the four of us knew these were an air-filling delay. Then Tom asked, "So what's the deal Pop?"

"It's like the old Myron Cohen joke about Morris the spy and The Big Black Dog." Tom, Patrick and I gazed at each other puzzled. Myron Cohen was one of The Old Man's favorite 1950s comics, a regular on The Ed Sullivan Show, a master at telling his jokes using a Yiddish accent. But we were baffled about the reference, given the circumstances. The Old Man, perceiving our bewilderment, launched into the tale.

"Israel intelligence sees that the Arabs are fitting to launch another war. So, they call in their best spy, Morris, to figure out what's going on. They send Morris secretly into the various Arab states neighboring Israel to dig up information. About six weeks later Morris returns with his report and meets with the Israeli leaders. They say, "So Morris, vat's going on?" "Oy" say's Morris, "It's terrible, just terrible. In the north, the Syrians have 150,000 men, 1,000 tanks, and 300 planes. In the east, the Jordanians have 100,000 men, 500 tanks, and 200 planes, and in the south, the Egyptians have 200,000 men, 1,500 tanks, and 500 planes." "Oy vey, this is very bad," said the leaders. "But Morris, what about in the vest, vat's in the vest?" "Oh, mien gott, dis is da vourst! This is very scary" says Morris. "In the vest, they gotta big black dog!"

Tom, Patrick and I chuckled politely, uncertain how this story fit The Old Man's situation. We said nothing. The Old Man lifted his head, studied us, and sensing our confusion said, "What I've got is the big black dog." The baseboard heater hummed, and we waited. He sat back, considered us again, and said, "I have to tell you, it's given me many dark nights of the soul." Now our understanding was complete. The three of us exhaled in unison. We were looking at the inevitable. The Old Man was going to die. We said nothing, just tight-lipped, jaws clenched. I held down my despair.

Then, The Old Man brought us back to the real world. He barked, "Hey, help me over to that thing… I gotta go" while pointing at a porta-potty on four aluminum legs sitting by the room's washbasin. I positioned myself on one side of The Old Man, Tom on the other, and we hoisted him from his place on the edge of the bed by putting our hands under his upper arms. I was shocked at how light and frail he was, this skeleton that'd been a super-being. We helped him shuffle over to the toilet; he opened the back of his hospital gown, spread his feet and sat. Again, Tom, Patrick and I glanced at each other, shocked speechless by the image of our once commanding father sitting there going to the bathroom in front of us. Heartsick and afflicted by this public humiliation, I turned my head.

The Old Man was never the nurturing, avuncular, pipe smoking, Robert Young Father-Knows-Best parent. He was a hard-nosed individual, a first generation, ass-out-of-the-pants, Irish-American kid whose intelligence and drive made him a success in book publishing. He once said to my mother, in response to her criticism of how tough he was with his three sons, "I'm not raising boys. I'm making men." The U.S. Marine Corps was perfect for The Old Man's personality and a template for his parenting skills. We paid heed to his commands and followed his orders without question or comment. We referred to him behind his back as "The Old Man," because that's what he called himself to stress a point: "Your Old Man knows what he's talking about." His use of the "Old Man" moniker came from his time in the Corps; it's a term of grudging respect enlisted men and subordinates use the term covertly when referring to commanding officers. We used it as well because it fit.

As I stood in front of The Old Man perched there on the portable toilet, I looked at the ceiling, I looked at my feet, I looked at the wall. Then, out of the corner of my eye, I glanced at him. He had assumed the elbows-on-knees pose, but this time he juggled a roll of toilet paper from one had to the other. He caught my eye, turned his face up to mine as I focused on him. Then he flipped the roll of toilet paper, and I grabbed it with both hands.

"You gotta help me here," he said.

My mind reeled. This wasn't happening. I was paralyzed. My father, a man I held in awe, a man whose physicality and his willingness to bring it red-hot kept me fearful most of my life, a man I knew as all-powerful, of towering strength... he wanted me to wipe his butt. I stood there dumbfounded my mouth open, my eyes lasering from Tom's eyes to Patrick's and back again, wordlessly begging for help, desperate and panicked.

With conviction, The Old Man said, "Hey, I wiped your ass when you were a baby. Now it's your turn to wipe mine."

Then a resolution hit me. Tom had always held the favored position as the eldest son in the family. For me, Tom had been coach, cheerleader, confidant, and consigliere, the responsible one. So, I flipped the roll of toilet paper to him and said, "You're the oldest. You do it." His eyes went full with a startled expression, and I let out a laugh. Once again, the onus was on the golden child. Then the laughter started from the four of us, and Tom did what he had to do.

Three weeks later, The Old Man awoke at 2 AM with a terrible ache in his chest. He was in a rented hospital bed in the second bedroom of his condominium. The doctors had said as the cancer advanced, there'd be growing heart discomfort. They prescribed liquid nitroglycerin and morphine mixed with juice to relieve the pain. My brother Patrick stayed with The Old Man, kept him company, and slept next to him on a cot. The three of us decided that one of us had to stay with him. We wouldn't leave him alone. Marion, The Old Man's second wife, hearing raised voices from his sick room, entered from her bedroom. When she understood The Old Man was in pain, she said she'd go to the kitchen to get his medicine and juice. As she turned to go, The Old Man, a 40-year dedicated Alcoholics Anonymous member and a rigorous follower of Bill W's steps, laughed and said, "Better make mine a double," an ironic reference to a double shot of booze. As Patrick held his hand, he laughed again, closed his eyes, and went to The Big Cocktail Party in the Sky.

> *"The leader of the band*
> *Is tired and his eyes are growing old*
> *But his blood runs thru' my instrument*
> *And his song is in my soul*
> *My life has been a poor attempt to imitate the man*
> *I'm just a living legacy*
> *To the leader of the band."*
> —Dan Fogelberg, 1981

Narrative Essay:

A Visit to the Tarlton Cross Mound
By Mark Wenden

ON A WARM DAY IN September 2009, I drove with my wife Kim along Route 159 in southern Ohio toward the small town of Tarlton. We had spent a long weekend in the area visiting historical sites. I have lived most of my life in Ohio, but my wife is from out of state, and I wanted her to become familiar with the history that had given me an unshakeable bond with Ohio since childhood. We had visited the Hopewell Cultural Center and Mound City Group, Adena House, Ohio's first governor's mansion, grilled hamburgers at the Seip Mound and read the somber monuments at the Logan Elm State Memorial. Now, as a last stop before returning to our home in the Columbus area, I wanted to show her the Tarlton Cross Mound. To our disappointment, we found that the park was shut down, not for the season, but permanently, and entrance was prohibited. But when we stopped in a small carryout in Tarlton to buy cold soft drinks for the ride home, we asked about the park, and the locals told us that people visit the mound all the time, and we should not worry about the chains and Keep Out sign.

So, we went back up the road and parked outside the gate and walked through the parking lot with its cracked asphalt overgrown with weeds, and through an old entry arch leading us to the path up to the mound. It was a short walk. The mound was small, as Indian mounds go, about 30 yards from the end of one arm of its cross shape to the other, with a circular depression at the center. A small metal Park Service plaque still stood next to it, pointing out that the orientation of the arms of the cross (the northern arm points directly north) gave evidence that its builders had some notion of astronomy and that no one knows which ancient culture actually built it. Other than that, the mound and its immediate vicinity showed no signs that anyone had cared for it for years. The trees nearby showed decades of unpruned growth, and vegetation threatened to overwhelm the mound itself in its dark and humid embrace. The appearance of the site had changed so radically, that it was only as we were turning to leave that I realized that

I had been here before and remembered how it had looked the last time I saw it.

The woods around the mound had been trimmed back and cleaned up then, and the grass on the mound itself was neatly mown. It was a crisp autumn day in 1961, and the late afternoon sun grazed the mound with cheerful rays, dappled by the swaying of branches dancing in the light breeze.

I was seven years old then, and as I stood at the end of the southern arm of the cross, my heart was in my mouth. As my mother fed the baby and looked after my four-year-old sister in the old Ford station wagon, my father had brought my older brother, older sister and me up the hill to the mound. We each had taken a position at the end of one of the arms of the cross and had been instructed in how to stand gravely at attention and in what to say as our turns came up. Our father began:

"I am Father North Wind. As my icy breath shakes the naked branches of the winter trees, children huddle in the lodges. The women go out only to gather firewood, and the men to set traps for beaver and mink, whose fur grows long with the cold, the better to keep the people warm."

Then my older sister recited her part, "I am Older Sister East Wind. My warm spring kiss brings blossoms and new birth to the land. The women plant corn and begin to gather berries as the mother bear leaves the den with her new cubs."

Next, it was my turn. I stammered and had to be reminded of my lines in the "solemn ceremony." "I am Younger Brother South Wind. I bring the white haze of summer, pierced by the cry of the cicada. The ears hang heavy on the cornstalks, and the braves set out on raiding parties to fight against our enemies!"

Finally, my older brother, though perhaps feeling too old to participate in this silliness, nonetheless spoke his lines well. "I am Older Brother West Wind. My clean and chilly breezes turn the fall leaves red and yellow and tell the deer to put on fat for the coming winter. The men hunt them and the women and children dry and smoke the meat and gather fruit and nuts for the hungry times to come."

As I walked with my wife down the hillside path away from the mound back out to our car by the road, some thoughts went through my mind. It had never occurred to me as a little boy that my father must have composed the contents of the "solemn Indian ceremony" in a matter of seconds as we arrived at the mound all those years ago. "Show an Irishman three things, and he'll spin you a tale," I thought to myself with a smile. My father had also been a teacher, one much-loved and respected by his students. Now, almost fifty years later, though the made-up ceremony seemed, in our more cross-culturally sensitive times, to be a somewhat condescending example of cultural appropriation, I realized at the same time how many significant ideas had been introduced or reinforced in that short, impromptu family activity at the mound: the importance of the cycle of the seasons to pre-industrial people, respect for the ideas of simpler societies, and how their beliefs and ceremonial lives may have meshed with the way they made their living, not to mention the value of learning your lines quickly and not being afraid to speak in front of a critical audience.

"How sad," I thought, "that the park is closed, and no other father will be able to enrich his children's lives in a similar way, giving them the sense that people long-forgotten, who were different from us, still matter somehow. At least, he won't be able to do it here."

My wife and I agreed that it was one of the best weekend trips we had ever taken together. The memory of the visits, nearly fifty years apart, still floats up into my consciousness now and then.

Persuasive Essay

The Overweight American
By Pat Fogarty

YOU DON'T HAVE TO BE A DOCTOR to recognize a health problem when you see one. If you watch the evening news, you'll notice Americans of all races and ages are disproportionally overweight. Doctors, research scientists, and others in the health community have come up with dozens of reasons for this apparent epidemic. Every year there seems to be a new theory that explains the ballooning problem.

Lack of exercise and the propensity of the American public to dine at fast food restaurants are often touted as the root of America's obesity problem. But these unhealthy habits are just two of the most obvious sources for the expanding problem. Health experts also cite—lack of sleep, depression, antibiotics, pesticides, skipping meals, portion sizes, artificial sweeteners, stress, food addiction and numerous other reasons for the increasing waistlines of the American public.

Well, everyone is entitled to an opinion and here's mine. The U.S. government started America on the road to plumpness more than fifty years ago with its trade embargo on Cuba. I know that's a difficult statement to swallow but let's look at the evidence. On October 19, 1960, the U.S. government stopped sending American manufactured products to Cuba, and Cuba stopped exporting sugar, rum, cigars and dozens of other items to America. In retrospect we can clearly see; the almost instantaneous shortage of sugar became the catalyst that eventually paved the way for America's obesity problem.

You can witness Americans morphing from thin to chubby, simply by going to almost any "Old Photos" website on the Internet. Photographs of Americans, especially of American children, taken before 1961 show a lean citizenry, and photos of Americans from the mid-1960's to the present confirm the progression of the heavier and heavier American.

So, what caused Americans to go from a healthy weighted society in 1961 to the gargantuan mass of humanity it is today? I say it was the result of American based companies changing the way they sweetened their products. With the abrupt stoppage of Cuban sugar entering the American market, commodity prices soared and the large sugar consuming companies like Coca-Cola, Pepsi, Hershey, and Kellogg switched from using sugar to using the less costly corn syrup.

For a while, it seemed like everyone was happy with the sugar switch. The food and beverage manufacturers' that switched to corn syrup were making huge profits. Some American farmers who had never planted a stalk of corn in the past were now planting corn in every field on their farm. Farmers were getting rich and the demand for corn kept soaring. The race was on to make as much corn syrup as quickly and as efficiently as possible.

Corn syrup was relatively simple to make. Gottlieb Kirchhoff invented a process for extracting the sweet syrup from corn in 1812. Back then, cornstarch and hydrochloric acid were mixed together and heated in a pressure cooker. Today chemists use more sophisticated methods and produce a variety of much sweeter products. High Fructose Corn Syrup is the most recognizable product in the group. But, depending on what processes are used to extract the syrup, and what part of the world you are living in, the basic product can have a dozen different names. Besides calling it High Fructose Corn Syrup, some of the other names used are Glucose-Fructose Syrup, Isoglucose, Fructose-Glucose Syrup, Dextrose, and High Fructose Maize Syrup.

With all the different names for the seemingly same product, people were getting confused and it wasn't long before health-conscious researches started publishing studies in medical journals that demonized corn syrup in all its forms. They made the argument that no matter how you chemically tweaked corn syrup, it would always cause you to gain weight and it would always be harmful to your health. Well, the corn syrup producers were not about to let that kind of talk go unchallenged. They hired the best scientific researchers money could buy and studies praising the syrup began appearing in medical journals around the world. But for every paper or study produced extolling their product, another one would appear condemning it. The barrage of arguments from both sides convinced some and baffled others. And today, the dispute continues. At this very moment, someone somewhere is saying, "When I was a kid Coca-Cola tasted much better and no one got fat because they didn't use corn syrup to sweeten it. They used real sugar."

Well, it took more than half a century, but it finally looks as if the big food and beverage corporations are listening to their customers. If you walk up and down the aisles of an American supermarket today, you'll see all sorts of products marked with signs stating they are made with pure cane sugar and that they contain neither Corn Syrup nor High Fructose

Corn syrup. So, if you really want to lose a few pounds, take the first step and read the labels. You might be shocked when you read some of the stuff they put in their products. I know I was stunned when I read the label on a box of salt. It read, "Ingredients: Salt, Sodium, Silco-aluminate, Dextrose, Potassium Iodide and Sodium Bicarbonate."

Finding Karen
By Dennis Royalty

Karen Stotts, you were just 17. I was 24. In the 43 years since our paths crossed at tornado-ravaged Monticello, I've wondered about your life. You endured so much.

IT WAS APRIL 3, 1974. I was a rookie news reporter based in West Lafayette, Indiana.

Notice I said "news" reporter. When *The Indianapolis Star* hired me that January, my hard news experience was minimal. I'd spent most of the previous three years covering sports for a paper that folded.

The Star assigned me to a one-person bureau, churning out news of northern Indiana. Short items mostly. Things like faculty raises granted at Purdue University, traffic fatalities and so forth. Break-in stuff. But April 3 seemed different. Ominous. Not a day for routine reporting.

It was raining hard, faucet-raining hard. Tornado warnings, too. So, I phoned my boss in downtown Indianapolis, State Editor Ernie Wilkinson.

"Denny, this looks real bad. Better get to the state police post."

Understandable. The West Lafayette State Police Post was the emergency nerve center for a dozen-county area.

I got drenched scrambling from my Chevelle to the door of the post. Roaring winds made an umbrella useless. Not only that, it was dark outside, twilight-like. Odd for 3:30 p.m.

Inside, activity swirled. Police radios chattered and pointed troopers to calls for help. This was no drill. I found a phone and called Ernie.

He was about to send me to one of the most jarring experiences of my life.

Ernest A. Wilkinson was a devoted, passionate newsman. By the time I began reporting to him in '74, he was 49 and had been State editor for Indiana's largest newspaper for 14 years. On the way up, he'd chased hundreds if not thousands of deadline stories.

Breaking news was Ernie's lifeblood. Now on his desk were reports of a potentially massive tornado outbreak.

Ernie knew that Rainsville, a tiny community near the state's western border, was being torn apart. That tornado originated in Illinois and was rampaging through his territory.

Ernie also realized that from his experience, most tornadoes travel from southwest to northeast. And 65 miles from where he was sitting, he had a reporter not far from the likely path. Me.

Ernie guessed where this powerful storm was headed. He laid a ruler across the state map he knew almost by heart. He was searching for the most heavily populated area on the frightening route.

"Denny, head for Monticello. Call from there."

I remember no other conversation at the state police post, where troopers were overwhelmed by an overworked switchboard. So it was back to my Chevelle, back to chase a tornado, an excited 24-year-old suddenly handed a major story.

Danger didn't occur to me. It was sometime around 4:30 p.m.

Monticello, Indiana, population 5,000-plus, is the White County seat, hugging the Tippecanoe River. A 40-50-minute drive should get me there. Emerging from the furious rainstorm, I learned through radio static that this looked to be a major outbreak. So be alert, be ready to take cover.

Still, I saw little evidence of tornado-like weather. Neck-craning toward a brighter sky, I saw only clouds sailing at a rapid clip.

Maybe halfway there, the sky turned an eerie green. And yet it was calm as I approached Monticello. The time was about 5:30 p.m.

On the outskirts, a curiosity. A few cars were parked where the highway became a city street, right in the traffic lane. They'd stopped without regard for anyone behind. There were no drivers or passengers in sight.

I soon found out why. Parking off the pavement at the edge of Monticello, I walked into a nightmare.

Huge trees were uprooted, many resting on top of roofs or ripped through them. Debris littered neighborhood yards and streets, including downed power lines.

Now I knew why it was impossible to drive further into the city.

I saw cars overturned and others shoved into front yards, where they plowed deep gashes into lawns. The few people I saw wore dazed, ashen looks. They were emerging from cover, discovering what had happened to their Monticello.

A widespread power outage froze electric clocks at 5:17 p.m. I grasped the chilling reality that the storm had hit fewer than 15 minutes before I arrived.

Ernie's directive had placed me moments away from the midst of one of the most destructive tornadoes in the 20th century.

Instead, I was about to chronicle its aftermath.

I captured all that I could in my notebook as I made my way to the center of the city.

Each block seemed more devastated than the last. Weaving through rubble, I was dumbstruck to find the 10-block business area looking like a war zone.

The county courthouse, a tall limestone and steel structure that dominated the local square for 80 years, was crushed inward. A direct hit ruined in one horrifying blow an architectural gem and symbol of rock-hard strength. Its clock tower was toppled, and roof destroyed.

My training taught me to keep focused. "Get the who, what, when, where, why, and how," I thought. Surely dozens had been killed and hundreds hurt.

I needed a voice of authority and found it in a makeshift state police command center. I was told there were many injured. Worst cases were rushed to a local hospital that thankfully wasn't obliterated.

After a couple of hours of gathering facts and quotes, I realized I must call Ernie by deadline. But this was long before cell phones. Phone lines were down for miles.

Racing to the Chevelle, I drove for a good half-hour before I spotted lights in a rural residence. Figuring there would be a working phone, I pleaded my way to its use and called in my notes.

I spent much of the next week in Monticello, filing news stories and using a tiny Instamatic camera to take the first front-page photo of my newspaper career.

My reporting focused on Monticello's portion of a much larger disaster. The combined storms eventually were characterized as a Super Tornado Outbreak.

Monticello, with approximately 350 injured and more than $100 million in damages (1974 dollars) had been struck by a tornado classified F4--winds reaching 200 mph--according to the National Weather Service. The big picture was 148 tornadoes affecting 13 states in an 18-hour period, the largest number of tornadoes recorded in a single event.

The Super Tornado outbreak resulted in 159 deaths (34 in Xenia, Ohio) and more than 6,000 injuries. Thirty of the 148 tornadoes rated the highest classifications, F4 or F5.

Somehow, there were only eight deaths in Monticello, despite being struck by a tornado that lay waste to an area of more than half-a-mile wide. The path of this particular tornado covered an incredible 121 miles in all, from Illinois to Rainsville to Monticello and beyond, although expert Ted

Fujita later determined there were actually two tornadoes on the path (one dissipated, quickly replaced by another).

Forty-three years later, numerous memories remain for me. One came from touring damage with a local official. Amid rubble on the courthouse lawn, I spotted a heavy block cornerstone. Noting its date, I assumed it was from the courthouse.

Not so. The official recognized the cornerstone from another smashed building, a few blocks away.

Two days after the storm, April 5, was the day I met Karen Stotts.

Once again, Ernie Wilkinson triggered the story. "Denny, you need to interview the girl who survived in the river. Get over to St. Elizabeth Hospital."

St. Elizabeth was not far from my office, in next-door Lafayette. Seventeen-year-old Karen had been taken there for treatment of a concussion.

State Police had told me about Karen's incredible—and heartbreaking—story in time for my coverage in that morning's newspaper. Initial facts were sketchy and inaccurate (including the spelling of her name. That happens in a breaking story of this magnitude). But the most tragic elements were accurate: Karen was a passenger in a van that happened to be passing through Monticello, crossing a bridge over the Tippecanoe River. The tornado snatched the van from the bridge and tossed it into the water, a drop of more than 50 feet.

Everyone else in the van, the driver and four other teenage girls, were killed. But Karen, seated in the rear, managed to swim out of the vehicle. Despite the fall and swift current, she struggled through the water to safety. A woman near the river bank answered her cries for help.

The day after the tornado struck, April 4, was when I used my inexpensive Instamatic to photograph the van as it was removed from the river by a large crane. I later learned that one of the young girls' bodies was still inside.

By the next morning, April 5, Ernie heard that Karen had been taken to St. Elizabeth. I would interview her there.

"I think it's a miracle that I'm alive," she told me, and that quote became the lead of my page one article on April 6. It was my first front-page story as a full-time news reporter.

Karen was propped in a seated position in her hospital bed. She looked small and delicate. And, she was calm. Surprisingly so, I thought.

As we spoke, divers were still searching for all of her fellow passengers except the young woman whose body was in the van pulled from the river.

Donald Richards, their seminary teacher, was driving Karen and the other teens back to Fort Wayne, where she was a senior at North High School. The group had participated in an educational tour at Nauvoo, Illinois.

"The weather was calm, but black outside," she said. "We turned right onto the bridge and the wind started blowing. At first, I thought it was hail that started hitting us (the van). But it must have been sticks and stones."

At that point, Richards told his students to get on the floor. But wind rolled the vehicle over and over and off the bridge.

She remembered hitting the water, nose down, the rear window exploding, feeling someone else under the water, and then "we were swept away in different directions."

The van landed about 10 feet from concrete bridge supports, but Karen was unable to reach the structures as she thrashed to stay afloat.

She reached a point "when I felt I was going to die and was ready to die, but something clicked in my mind and I knew I wouldn't." Rolling on her back helped. Karen saw houses and tried to make it toward them. Finally, her head bumped a branch. She grabbed it and pulled herself to shore.

Reviewing my yellowed news clipping from 1974, I wondered if our roles had been reversed, would I have been as composed as the brown-haired teen I interviewed—only two days after it happened.

I closed my '74 article as it had begun—by letting Karen speak.

"I love each and every one of them very much," she said. "They are with the Lord. When He calls people, that's the way it is. He just didn't want me to go now.

"Someday, I'll be with them again."

Retirement brings the gift of time. This is what ended my decades-long excuse for not contacting Karen.

In June 2017, I Googled "Karen Stotts and tornado." There I found "In the Path of the Tornado," an article written by Karen Stotts Myatt and published in 2008 by *Ensign*, a magazine for The Church of Jesus Christ of Latter-Day Saints (LDS).

We connected on Facebook and spoke by phone several days before she turned 61. She called from her car, stronger of voice but with the same calm, straightforward manner.

After 43 years, we had another interview.

I learned that the young woman who converted to the LDS faith just eight months before her fateful trip went on to do missionary work and has been an LDS educator for 21 years. Karen teaches courses including college level. Donald Richards would no doubt be proud.

Karen lives in Sandy, Utah, about 20 miles south of Salt Lake City. She married Ronald Myatt a little more than five years after Monticello. Their "three beautiful kids" are 35, 33, and 31.

Are you OK, Karen?

"I have my moments," she said. "I still have some PTSD—getting worse, actually. I suspect that's because of my age. But I've never put this subject in the 'don't want to talk about it' category.

"It was difficult to stay in Fort Wayne," she said. "All the families (of victims) cried when they saw me." So she moved first to Salt Lake, then California, then back to Utah. But she keeps in touch with two of the families.

Karen recalls initially being taken to the hospital in Monticello. There, she was released because so many people had cuts and broken bones, while she had no readily apparent serious injuries. But the next morning, good Samaritans she stayed with noticed Karen forking a countertop instead of her scrambled eggs. That's how she wound up at St. Elizabeth, treated for a concussion.

Turns out she also pulled back muscles, an injury that still bothers her. "But I've led a productive life. I decided long ago you don't get over anything like this. It's always going to be with me. God helps you get through it."

She's never returned to Monticello. She was invited, but it didn't work out timewise. She did return to Illinois with her family in 2002 for the dedication of the new Nauvoo Temple, which has great significance for the LDS church and its members.

The original temple was destroyed in the 1800s, most of it by fire and the rest, ironically, by a tornado. The church bought land in Nauvoo in 1937, determined to continue its presence in the land where Joseph Smith and Brigham Young played key roles in the origins of Mormonism.

Karen wrote in the magazine that she carried an unnecessary burden of guilt for many years "because I was spared from death while four talented and lovely young women and our seminary teacher were not. Now, I felt healed. I knew I had been meant to remain on earth to finish my course."

I asked whether I had caused her further pain with our interview on April 5, 1974.

No. In fact, it took a while for Karen to remember me in our initial Facebook conversations.

As someone who lived through unspeakable tragedy, she had this advice for professionals like me:

"Sensitivity," she urged. "I cringe when I see how victims are interviewed on TV...questions get asked that reach the point of being crass."

That's not me, Karen, or at least not the journalist I've tried to be. I wish you the best, and I so appreciate the opportunity to speak with you. Again.

I'm Going to Hell
By Tom Spirito

IT WAS MY SECON SEASON working at The Roundup Ranch Resort located in the Catskill Mountains of New York. The dude ranch was nestled in a horseshoe-shaped valley, on three thousand acres of green pastures and forest. I had been promoted the previous Fall from "pilot" to dude wrangler. You may be wondering what does a "pilot" do at a dude ranch. "Pilot" was the slang term for the barn boy because his prime mission was to scoop up all the horse poop and "pile it" here and "pile it" there. Yup, I piled it here, there and everywhere for the entire previous season. But now, I was a "Catskill Cowboy." This was the fulfillment of my youthful fantasies, born out of a misspent childhood in front of the boob tube, jam-packed with rootin' tootin' Hollywood Western action, courtesy of Gene, Hoppy, The Ranger, and Roy. Cowboy was actually, pronounced "Kaboy" in New Yorkese. One of my favorite guests dubbed me with that moniker one day when he said, "Tom, you're a real Kaboy." I took this as a compliment, thought it sounded kind of catchy, and so "The Catskill Kaboy" was born.

The Summer season of 1968 didn't get busy until schools closed around the metropolitan New York, New Jersey area. But before the schools released their howling mobs, they took them on their class trips. Roundup Ranch was the day trip destination for one inner-city Catholic school that I called "Our Lady of Perpetual Saddle-sores." They would arrive in two school buses loaded with children, ranging in age from too young to not old enough, escorted by several nuns. Yes, NUNS! Now being a naive, young man of Italian descent and raised in the Roman Catholic faith, I had a great respect for nuns. Correction make that a great fear of NUNS! The sisters ran roughshod over these children of the asphalt jungle. After deconstructing much of the ranch facilities, the nuns assembled the little darlings into groups of about thirty and marched them down to our stable for their first experience on horseback. Well, I knew the drill for mounting dudes pretty thoroughly by this time and was confident that although a challenge, we could handle this "cast call for The Lord of the Flies" without a hitch.

What I wasn't prepared for was that the nuns would be accompanying the kids on the trail ride. Now, this was 1968. Nuns were still wearing the traditional attire from the top of their white mitered crown to the black veiled robes cinched at the waist with rosary beads and a crucifix, right down to their little black granny shoes. And just to make it interesting, we didn't have a mounting block. Now children were easy to mount up. You just put your hands under each armpit and up they went.

Adults of varying sizes were a bit more challenging. First, you'd help them put their left foot in the stirrup. Second, you hold the reins and brace the saddle with your left hand. Third, have the rider grab hold of whatever they could reach with their hands. This often included the wrangler. Fourth, gently cup your right arm under the prospective rider's butt. Fifth, lift them up and into the saddle. By the numbers, this was almost always a pretty slick and quick operation known as "dude launching." On this fateful day, I drew the plum assignment. My nun was about 4 feet tall and almost just as wide—not exactly equestrian friendly to put it kindly. Not that there aren't many talented and skilled riders in the plus weight range, I'm no lightweight myself. However, this was not a problem of physicality, but of culture and upbringing. I was going to have to TOUCH A NUN! Not just touch her but manhandle her. I tried to dig way down for courage, thinking of the examples of all those WWII and Western movie heroes. I smiled and said, "Howdy Sister." Her eyes bored through me just like an alien heat ray from a sci-fi movie and I knew I'd seen this horrible thing before. I felt that Nun's ruler come down on my psychological knuckles, just as it had so many years ago on my actual knuckles. My mind kneeled and prayed for a miracle or at least a little mercy. Why didn't we have a mounting block, a ladder, a forklift, something? Why hadn't we taught these horses to kneel?! Clearly, the under the armpit heave-ho wasn't going to work. The adult mounting procedure by the numbers would have to do. Lord knows how I got her foot, that little, black, granny shoed foot, into the stirrup. Inspired, I placed the reins in my teeth, a la John Wayne True Grit style. I knew I would need both hands to propel Sister to escape velocity. The Sister's reach enabled her to just barely grab the stirrup fender on either side. I could see she was going to be of marginal assistance during the launch procedure.

We had arrived at the moment of truth. I couldn't feel my right arm. It was moving as if a trained reflex had taken over, like the soldiers that jump up out of their foxholes and move forward into no-man's land and I was definitely in NO-MAN'S LAND! I cradled her butt in the crook of my right arm and gave a mighty upward boost with the help of my left hand on her left cheek. At this point, time seemed to stand still as my observable surroundings became a surreal, disorienting, blur of swirling, blinding, black veils circling my head. A jarring impact to my left temple jerked me back to the unfolding horror of my situation. Sisters' crucifix had just bounced off my noggin' with a slightly hollow "THUD!"

Suddenly I heard a new auditory sensation, akin to the crack of doom, the Sister "GIGGLED!" Oh God, I'd touched a NUN's butt and she GIGGLED! Oh Lord, let it be no more than a tickle. Desperately I thought that perhaps I could find salvation in the confessional. A voice deep inside me said, "Fat chance there "Kaboy." I had broken the Eleventh Commandment: "Thou Shalt Not Touch A Nun's Butt and Make Her Giggle." It was no use. I knew I was lost. For sure, I was goin' to hell. No ifs, ands, or BUTTS!

Nineteen Forty-Four
By Joseph Babinsky

Excerpts from the Memoir: "Climb the Mountain – A Path Taken

IT WAS NOT THE BEST OF TIMES. In our family, it was a horrible time. As for me, a nine-year-old boy, it was a nightmare. This was the day everyone cried, especially mom, dad and my older siblings. If I had looked around (which I didn't dare do) I might have seen other people in the room also crying. I did hear the noise—people blowing their nose and loud moans.

At the front of the room, there was black cloth draped over a table. His photograph was on the table. Large baskets of flowers were on the floor. We were in church—the church where my father was the pastor. I was sitting in the front row with my family.

I really didn't understand what was going on. I only knew that Charles, my favorite brother, was killed during the War in 1944.

We first heard about the death of Charles at Christmas. I came into the living room and saw my mother crying. She was wiping away tears with her handkerchief, and with her other hand, she was removing ornaments from our family Christmas tree. Dad was standing near the fireplace, holding a yellow paper in his hand. He was crying really hard. Never saw anything like this before. They received a telegram from the War Department. It was news telling us that Charles was killed in action. All the kids heard the commotion and were told what happened.

After church, we went home and ate a meal. I recall that all my siblings were home. Two brothers were still in the army; they were home. When we finished eating, dad started a conversation about what each of us would do when the war was over. The older ones knew what they were going to do. They spoke first and explained plans for their lives. Several in the family were in high school and told their plans to go to college. Everyone but me was standing.

I sat in the high-back chair and tried to hide. I wanted my dad to forget that I was in the room. I was wrong. He turned and spotted me sitting in the big chair. *Ghee whiz, what was I going to say? Don't ask me, please!*

Dad looked directly at me: "Alright, Joey, you're last. What about you? What do you want to do when you grow up?"

To tell the truth, the first thing that I wanted to say was that I dreamed to be a soldier, like Charles, and go shoot people—shoot them like they shot and killed my brother.

I didn't say this. No way! I squirmed in the chair, and merely stammered: "I don't know."

Memories of this time period are vague, not only because I was a young boy, but I have a lot of mixed feelings and emotions about this period in my life. I'm telling it here only because of what happened after the Memorial Service at the West Side Hungarian Church located in Buffalo, New York. The thing that happened was the question asked by my dad. His words stuck with me the rest of my life. In the years ahead, what he said lingered and became a huge influence.

This narrative is purposely placed at the beginning—it serves as a prologue to this book. As the story develops, it will be shown that the question asked was remembered and remained an abiding presence to assist various decisions and changes during my long life. The death of Charles, and the question asked by my father, merged into one experience and colored my life in such a way that it followed me both as a shadow and a guide.

Within the story I tell, an answer to the question slowly emerges.

No Common Abiding Place

By the time I wanted to know more about my family, we were all old—even me. When I started to write this book (2014), all but three had already died.

A sister, nearly ninety, offered to provide information about the early life of our family. When she began to tell family stories, she quickly realized that buried memories remembered brought on sleepless nights. Thus, she did the thing she felt best for her to do, which meant that she quit sharing stories with me.

At this writing, I have one additional sister still living. Dorothy is close to me in age; our birthdays are only fifteen months apart. Many years ago, she made it clear that I didn't know our family history. We were having a conversation with a mutual friend. The talk drifted to our family, and I mentioned: "there were twelve in our family, seven boys and five girls." Dorothy quickly interrupted and corrected me: "No, that's not right! There are eleven in our family!" I laughed and answered: "Dorothy, why don't you ask mom how many children she had!" Mother was still alive, but to my knowledge, Dorothy never asked mom.

Over the years I did what research I could. I found that Dad kept records of the family in his Bible. He recorded the date, name and place of birth of each child. There are twelve births listed in his Bible. He wrote a note that a daughter died one day after birth, July 2, 1924.

For the longest time, I carried the opinion that we had two families. There were four in the first family, born between 1916 and 1920, three boys and one girl. In the second family, there were eight—four girls and four boys, born between 1924 and 1935. The two families were separated by four and a half years, a period when no children were born.

It is a mystery when and how I became aware of the number in our complete family. A few weeks after I was born the two eldest sons left home for good. One brother went off to college, and the other went to live with his aunt, my mother's sister. I did not have much of a memory of either of them until 1944 when they came home for the funeral of Charles. Even then, they seemed more like strangers or distant relatives than brothers. And the same thing applies to my eldest sister. She left home when I was only one-year-old. And the third brother left home when I was three. So, in essence, my view of our family was that there were seven of us—three brothers and three sisters.

There might be more to this story than I am telling, but I'll never know. I say this because I heard my sisters whisper things about the subject of children, and why there were so many births in our family. I was a snoopy boy, and they probably didn't see that I was close enough to hear their conversation. I heard them say that mom went to a doctor to ask how she might stop having more children. I do not know when this took place, or if it happened at all. If mom did go to a doctor and ask advice about birth control, when did she do it? Did mom do this after the first four were born (what I call the first family)? Perhaps she did it after I was conceived and took matters in her own hands and stopped having sex with dad—the only birth control information she had. I'm guessing, of course. I say this because it helps explain, to an extent, why I never felt that I was really wanted.

I had a curiosity to know more about our family origins, and when older turned to genealogical research for answers. I already knew that we were Hungarians, and I wanted to know if we were related to the famous neurologist, Dr. Josef Babinski, born in France. My oldest brother, Elmer, told the story which he called a family legend. He said that there were three brothers that lived in Poland, and during a threat of war they fled Poland. One brother went to France; he became the father of the famous doctor. A second brother went to Czechoslovakia and drifted to Brazil. The third brother went to Hungary and became the grandfather of our dad. I like this story and often tell it, but my genealogical search did not prove it. On the other hand, the research did not prove the legend false. It is mentioned here as a story, and it is the way that I tell it when asked by anyone about my surname.

My dad was an immigrant; this much I know to be true. He came to America in 1910 from Hungary, the place of his birth. My mother, Julia (Kayati), was born in Youngstown, Ohio, but both her parents (Andrew Kayati and Suzanna Pastor) were born in Hungary.

Dad was a teacher when he lived in Hungary, and this is what he did for a living when he came to America. Later, he attended theological school, and was ordained a Christian minister. After several different cities and churches, he moved his family to South River, New Jersey. They lived here during the heart of the Great Depression, and when things grew desperate, he found a solution. When I was two years-old, dad once again decided to move the family. Where? The family moved to an orphanage in Pennsylvania.

His plan was supposed to be a move for the good of the entire family. What began as a good idea became a nightmare for nearly everyone—at least for me it did.

A question could be asked as to why my father chose to move the family to an orphanage. The only answer I am able to provide is what little I know of the early life of our family, gathered in pieces and bits from older brothers and sisters and this, coupled with the slim knowledge I possess of the social and economic situation existing during the 1930s in the United States. One answer I have come up with is simple, and it is not an exaggeration: Our family was poor—very poor.

The older sister, mentioned above, shared information with me about the conditions of our family life while living in South River. Our dad was the pastor of a small church that had few members. He did not have additional employment and source of income. Many times, the people of his congregation had no funds to share with the church, and to pay his salary. The people did the best they could, and often gave help only in the form of food. They gave the family things like apples, peaches, pears and fresh garden vegetables—carrots, beets, potatoes.

This same sister said that when we arrived at the orphanage, we were immediately instructed that the children were not permitted to address our parents as mom, dad or in any other personal way. For the benefit of those who were truly orphans, we were taught to call dad, "Mr. Teacher," and mom, "Mrs. Teacher". We became orphans—though, of course, in name only.

When I consider the stories about our family, a move to an orphanage seemed to be my dad's only choice. Knowing this makes it understandable but provides little relief to the young child that I was. Eighty years later I can't imagine a two-year-old child not saying *mommy*. How can you undo a boy's relationship with his mom and dad? Who suckled him when he was sad or sick? Did she take the boy along with her when she went to her duties as the cook for the orphanage? Was the little child scolded (or worse, punished) when he was heard to say *mommy* or *daddy*?

The stories of my "beginnings" tell a great deal about certain factors that went into the formation of my basic personality, and the underlying loneliness and unsettledness that I have experienced throughout my life. I make no attempt to speculate how it was for the ten siblings older than me. However, I cannot help but wonder what their experiences were. When I study the list of births in our family, dates, places born, I see the number of times the family moved from place to place, city to city, and each child still very young, I sense that we all share a common thing, namely, we had no stable home—no roots. Our common root, in addition to the same father and mother, is a picture of a family continually on the move, similar to gypsies.

I do think that if each sibling were asked to tell his or her story, I guarantee that eleven very different books would be written. This is as it should be. Even though we were members of the same biological family, we are, after all, individuals, and each one has a story to tell. This is my story.

The Bus Stop

I would have enjoyed having him as my older brother. I was young, of course, but I saw Charles as a giant, not just physically tall, but tall and strong. After I grew older I discovered that he was also intelligent, an honor student in high school, and an outstanding athlete. Also, I learned that he helped the family by working as a salesman in a clothing store, Riverside Men's Shop, located in our neighborhood near the Niagara River in Buffalo.

Our family was devastated by the news that he was killed in action— mom, dad, my brothers and sisters, other relatives, members of our church, many friends and neighbors.

The scene is clear in my memory. When I heard the news, I ran upstairs to my bedroom. I threw myself on the bed, cried out loud and yelled: "No, no! It is a lie! It is not true! You'll see; he'll come home." I refused to believe that Charles was really gone.

Often, I sat alone outside on the front steps of our home, watching for a city bus. I waited and watched for a bus to come along on Tonawanda Street, and stop near our house. I knew that I would see Charles get off the bus, smile and wave to me. That's what I believed would happen. I believed it strongly and knew without a doubt that he was coming home. They tried, but nobody could convince me otherwise.

There were two funerals for Charles: The first was a Memorial Service, which was soon after we received the news in the telegram that he was killed in action. This was the same time that my father asked the question: *What are you going to do when you grow up?*

The second funeral happened years later. His body was shipped home in a sealed casket. I was one of the pallbearers. When I touched the casket, I knew his body was not inside. That's why I used to sit on the steps and watch for a bus. I did this for a long time. But it never happened. Charles did not come home. He never came home. And one day, I quit watching city buses on Tonawanda Street. Instead, I watched the girls walk by. But that is a story for another day.

Dad Knew Mickey Mantle
By Tom Spirito

My Father was not a fountain of parental advice. I have often noted that the only bit of useful knowledge he passed on to me was, "Son, be true to your teeth or they'll be false to you." He would expound on this gem of wisdom with a solemn look and a slight whirl of his right-hand index finger skyward as if these words had been inspired by the almighty and passed personally down to him, and on to me. He would then look down at me, smile, laugh and give me a big hug. After decades of infections, cavities, pulled teeth, and gum surgery, I have got to admit, he got that one right. But who knew that would be the one and only bit of advice to me that he would get right? I could have saved myself a lot of pain, and money, if I had only paid heed to that pearl of wisdom; that one pearl.

Actually, I do remember a day when Dad got it unbelievably, almost mystically right. Mom had passed away sixteen months before and I was slowly realizing our lives were increasingly "going off the rails." I was feeling insecure and in total denial of the many ways my life was changing. Our future seemed uncertain and frightening to this coddled and spoiled only child. Mom's death had replaced me as the center of our universe and left us with a black hole in our lives.

It was Saturday, October 10th, 1964, a classic Fall day in New York. Dad and I were attending the third game of The World Series at Yankee Stadium between our Yanks and the Saint Louis Cardinals. Yankee Stadium, that high temple of America's favorite pastime, the holy house of my boyhood heroes, was bathed in sunshine in all its hallowed majesty. It even smelled glorious. We were seated in the mezzanine seats along the third base line. It was late in the game, and Dad and I had managed to cover the floor under our seats with peanut shells, Dixie cups, and hotdog holders. The Yankees and Saint Louis were tied at the bottom of the ninth one to one and the fans were loudly buzzing in anticipation as the Yankees left the field. The air became electric when it was announced that Mickey Mantle would be the first batter for The Yankees. The crowd bellowed its approval. I stopped eating and sat fixed at the edge of my seat in anticipation. Mickey, my hero, the guy on the pedestal, at the center of the altar I worshiped at was coming up to bat. Out of the blue, Dad stands up, grabs my hand and says, "Let's go. Mantle's going to hit a home-run, and we can beat the traffic outta the Bronx." I stared up at him in astonishment and blurted, "What, go now?" Dad grabbed my hand and pulled me up off my seat. We rushed to the stairs. Down we hustled to the ground floor and stood in the alley right behind home plate. Mickey was in the batter's box by this time taking a few practice swings. To this day, burned into my retinas, is the image of that large, black number 7 centered beneath those broad shoulders. And then they were in motion, rotating quickly. It was the first pitch to Mickey and the last of the game. A loud crack of the bat reverberated back to Dad and me. The ball lofted high towards the right-field bleachers and was gone in the upper deck. The entire stadium was on its feet yelling, howling, whistling in one cataclysmic roar. My Father jerked me backwards and we sprinted for the exit leaving Yankee Stadium with 67,000 screaming fans and Mickey's triumph behind. My brain was swimming. As we dashed to our car, I kept looking in awe at my Father, and repeating, "How did you know, how did you know?" Dad just smiled and pointed that swirling index finger skyward.

We certainly did beat the traffic out of the Bronx that day. I'm sure most folks would say it was just a lucky hunch inspired by the fear of getting stuck in one more colossal traffic jam on The Cross Bronx Expressway. I could never see it that way. For me, a vulnerable 14-year-old, it was one of the most wonderful and amazing days I ever spent with my Father.

After Mom died, Dad struggled with the loss of, in his words, "The love of my life." He remained single to the day he died, thirty-three years later. As a single father trying to raise a son, he got so many things wrong. But on that Fall day in Yankee Stadium, my Dad knew Mickey Mantle and what he was about to do. It was a day that all Fathers should pray to have with their child. It helps me to forgive, but not to forget.

We tell ourselves stories in order to live.
—*Joan Didion*

The World According to Arnie
By Greg Picard and Wendy Picard Gorham

NONE OF THEM ARE 'blacks and whites' anymore," Arnie Blusten spit out around his cigar. He stood to peer at the vehicle through the only dirt-encrusted pane that was not replaced by plywood in the window frame. Mavis Blusten sat in a vinyl settee looking more like an overfull sack of potatoes than a woman in her early forties. When she rose to cross the bare wooden floor, the lumps of cellulite at the hem of her shift showed imprints of the buttons used to tuck the Naugahyde to the padded chair frame. Sulfurous bruises, tinged the same color of the chair's black vinyl, sagged beneath her left eye.

"What do you suppose they want way out here at this hour?" Mavis' voice was a thin and reedy squawk. Together they both watched as two men in khaki climbed out of the white with green four-wheel drive GMC. A stripe slashed boldly across its door with a government seal centered on the decal of a six-pointed star. The setting sun off to the west cast shadows across the narrow track of Boulder Creek Road."Whatever it is, you can bet it isn't something you need to bother yourself with!"

Arnie eyed the fading bruise on his wife's cheek. "Now get in the kitchen and make dinner. I'll take care of this."

Yellowed Sycamore leaves swirled and began to dust the earth with a warning of impending winter. The San Diego County deputy's companion had a different park service patch and badge. They were just stepping onto the aged and creaking wooden deck when Blusten yanked open the door. "This here's private property! You'd best be moving on down the road! You got no cause to be messin' with me!"

"Mr. Blusten, we hate to bother you, but we need to talk to you about your son, Jack." The tall deputy put on his friendliest smile. "It seems he was involved in some trouble down in Cuyamaca." Here the smile faltered, "We have him in custody on a warrant for murder charges. Could we come in?" In response, a gust of late fall wind caught the screen door, and it yawned open. The return spring "twanged" to its limit and the peeling wood frame cracked against the siding. Blusten shuffled back a half stride.

Arnie and Mavis Blusten had lived in the hills behind North Peak for 16 years. At sixteen, Mavis had their first and only child, Jack. Arnie spent most of his time at the Julian Hotel as their part-time handyman and at the Wrong Branch as the town drunk. Mavis was ill-equipped to give Jack the proper upbringing he needed, but she tried to give him some love and attention. Mostly, it was too little and too late. He grew up a lonely child, spending his first five years in the very same cabin in the woods the deputy and the park ranger now stood. Their nearest neighbor was eight miles away. All that changed when he started school.

He approached kindergarten with the same intensity that he approached his Teddy bear. Deprived of the contact with others his age by life in the virtual wilderness, he literally assaulted other children in order to get their attention. The school bus was not a frightening new experience, but rather a wonder of new "toys" with which to play.

The deputy stood while the ranger sat on the vinyl settee. Arnie tried to make the wiring in his alcohol worn brain connect. "How could Jack have murdered anybody, why that's as silly as saying I done that!"

"Actually, Mr. Blusten, we're talking more than that." The ranger had deep creases in his forehead from time in the sun, and the tan was peeled raggedly along his hairline as he removed his Stetson hat. "My name is Chris Becker. I work in the park, and I needed to let you know that it would appear that from the evidence that Jack is responsible for the murder and sexual assault of one of the maids at the Lakeside Motel cabins...a young Hispanic lady just here in this country.

"My son don't know no Mex wetbacks. He wouldn't associate with that kinda trash!" By now, the cigar ash had collapsed on Blusten's yellowed undershirt.

The balding deputy leaned forward, and the leather from his Sam Browne Belt creaked. "We're pretty sure the semen swab samples will paint a different picture, I'm afraid, as will the tissue samples under three of the victim's fingernails. The witness statements put him there coming out of the room she was cleaning."

Ranger Becker broke in. "He asked that you be notified. I expect you'll want to talk to him at the County Jail."

Arnie rubbed his sausage-like fingers across the two-day growth of beard, not sure what to make of all this. He looked toward the kitchen and wondered vaguely what Mavis had started for dinner.

Mavis was a good cook, he thought to himself.

My Casita
By Christy Powers

I WILL NOT BE RETURNING to my place by the sea, the place I call My Casita. It was a dream that became a reality and now it will be stored away tenderly in my memory.

I have another month here and I must use it well. But there is reality to deal with and that detracts from the magic. Taxes and newsletters take energy.

This place began as a dream, an unreality, a moonbeam worth grasping. Walking around the vacant garage, above which houses a dream too obscure, I pictured myself within those walls overlooking the ever-changing water and placing wonderful words into stories that would secure my place on the bookshelf.

I had always longed for this kind of opportunity of time, of place, of peace, and of nature. To me, it would prove whether I had that skill with words that could make a difference.

What I learned through it all, is what I have always known, but have shoved aside. One does not need a place except in the heart, and soul. and mind. My place is where I am and while changing my home may change the outlook for a minute or an hour, it does not change what I am, nor who I am, nor how well I write.

I love my place here overlooking the bay. I listen night and day to the sounds that I do not hear at my other place. The birds here are different and the trees have a different sound from the wind. The wind blowing in off the sea has a personality all its own.

Walking along the beach, I see and hear and smell the world around me in a way foreign to those from the world of mountains or lakes or deserts. Strolling on the beach can open my eyes if I will allow them to open. My early morning and evening walks help to infuse me with the smells and sounds and pictures that I treasure. My hope is; if I store them deeply enough and remember to call upon them frequently, the misty fragrance smells and the tidal lapping sounds of small waves will stay with me until my final days.

The fact is; this place which I love severs my life and keeps me from really belonging anyplace. I often think of the things that I am missing at my other place, like spending spring in my garden and waiting for the first robin to arrive. Or the joy of watching the leafing of the trees outside my sunroom window. I love it there. And thankfully, my life there is not one of total solitude. I allow the distractions of phone and news and email to chop my day like garlic on a cutting board.

I also love *My Casita*, the place overlooking the bay. But the financial burden is far too great, and I worry and wonder why I ever thought I could do such a thing in the first place. I am grateful for the years of having *My Casita*, my place overlooking the bay. I have loved it and will store the view of the bay in my mind as I travel through the rest of my life. And, if in my writings, I should ever feel stuck for words, I will remember my place by the sea. And, in my mind, I shall sit in front of the window by the sea and watch the changing mood of the water through the trees now bare that reach skyward in the awkwardness of youth. I will listen and smell the world that I loved and experience glorious thoughts, except they'll fade like a dream in the wind when the reality of money and taxes and newsletters come to attack its magic.

If I thought it would be the answer, I could move here I suppose. But I know I would grow stale and lazy with this peace because that is my nature. I would have to work away from my place at the window if I lived here and that would chip away at the magic.

During the next month, I will suffer through the reality of taxes, the bustle of another holiday and the creation and distribution of another newsletter. Will I have time enough to dream and finely chisel the memories I want to take with me? This is my place and I love it here. But I do not belong here and my life is on hold waiting for my return. I have never had such a dream as this Casita before that I was able to turn into reality. The change from dream to reality spoils the magic.

I do not really know whether I am sad about this dream turned into reality. New people have come into my life and they will remain in my life. The way of life is different here and yet the same. It is the differences that I want to cling to and dream about and always remember.

In a month I will pack up and move on. I will cry a little and wonder if I should have done this in the first place. It was never a practical idea and mostly I am the practical sort. I will always be grateful that this opportunity presented itself and I dared to grasp it and cling to it through all the times of self-punishment and condemnation that come with allowing a dream to become reality. I hope I can hang on to the magic, the view from this window, the wonder of the world as I walk the beach in the morning and evening. The gentle breezes that float in off the sea and the fine mist from the small waves make certain that my walks are never the same from one time to the next.

But mostly I hope I have learned that to write is a gift of the heart and the soul. If the talent be mine, I need to practice and nurture and dream my dreams wherever I may be. The place is inside of me. The magic is inside of me. The love to write is balanced with the need to write. If this gift be mine, never let me make an excuse of place or time or worldly commitment. If this gift be mine, may I use it wisely.

I will not be returning to *My Casita* that I love except through the magic of imagination, dream, and memory. In my heart and in my soul, I know I made the right decision, but still, I feel as if part of me will always remain at *My Casita* by the sea.

Does that mean I will not write? Only if I cease to live. For to write and to live are one.

Pussy Cats
By Joe DiBuduo

Stealthy paws silently fall as felines strut onto my lawn of sand, a Siamese's drawn-out meow heralds, throughout the cat hood, telling all who hear, that my yard is the place to go, to show their glee, that they can pee for free on my turf. Cat trinkets are left for me, covered in tiny mountains of sand like miniature burial mounds.

"You're not welcome here," I shout and chase them away. But they soon return to use their outhouse made of sand, where they don't have to pay a damn thing, to do what nature demands. A dog is what I need. I go to the pound and put a kitten in my hand, to see which dog hates cats more than me. Pitiful pups crammed into stalls, unfit for a dog, or even a cat, they're all waiting to be gassed. Aroused by my human scent their adoption hopes rise. They beg to be saved, with made up yelps, and all forget about the feline in my hand. Except, Molly, a sixty-pound white Lab, she snaps, snarls, and tries with all her might to get her lunch at first sight of the cat I hold.

She's the one I want, I tell the keeper of these surplus pets. I'm happy to think that my home turf will be cat free, once Molly comes home with me. I stop at the store to get what she needs, a bone, a blanket, a bed, a bag of food. I brush and bathe her in my tub, getting her ready to show those cats, they no longer rule. Rough, ready and smelling sweet from doggy shampoo, we sit and wait until a Persian saunters into my yard and begins building a burial mound in the sand. My heart fills with glee as I point at the Persian and declare, "Get him, Molly."

She can't wait to get out the gate, barking, and snarling, her feet slip on the floor as she tries to push through the door. I fumble with the latch in my rush to free this horrible hound onto my monument strewn lawn. To show those cats, a beast now lives here. Finally, the door bursts open, a ball of white fur speeds in the direction of the cat lazily scratching through the sand. A hairy back balls up to the sky, claws extend, a screaming yawl that scares even me, stops Molly in her tracks. She turns around and heads back to the entry in fearful flight, with an apparition from every dog's nightmare in hot pursuit. Yelping in fear, she burst through the door that I barely close in time, to stop the demon cat from coming through. Shivering from fear Molly sits there, ashamed that as a dog, she is nothing but a pussy cat.

Lest I Forget
By Carol A. Rotta

DUST MOTES FLOATED LAZILY in the afternoon rays of California-sunshine that poured through the windows, across the blue Formica table top, and onto the darker blue-patterned linoleum floor. I loved this corner of the cheery yellow and white kitchen that mother referred to as, the "breakfast nook." Tucked at one end of the room, it was always pleasant, especially when the sun was shining through the large windows facing southwest at the front of the house.

I flopped in one of the S-shaped chairs upholstered in bright yellow vinyl and tucked my feet under me. I glanced at the delft-blue and white Dutch clock that hung at the end of the upper cabinet. *It's almost time for my program to start.* Daddy had already looked over my homework. He'd given me an ultimatum in September when I started seventh grade, "You can't listen to any of your radio programs 'till you've finished all your homework." And that meant weekends, too.

Turning around, I reached over and turned the knob of the small, black rectangular-shaped radio that sat against the white tiled sink. I listened to the announcer extol the virtues of the product that sponsored the program, then the familiar deep, rolling laugh from Throckmorton P. Gildersleeve— *The Great Gildersleeve.* I smiled with pleasure and chuckled right along with him and squirmed to settle more comfortably in my seat, ready to be entertained for the next half-hour.

Suddenly to my annoyance, an unfamiliar, somber-sounding voice cut in with the announcement, "We interrupt this program to report the Japanese have bombed Pearl Harbor." The program came back on and I was able to catch up on the plot of the story as it continued.

Again, there was the announcement, "We interrupt this program to report the Japanese have bombed Pearl Harbor."

The broadcast resumed, but with the same intrusion continued. Soon, I'd lost the thread of the storyline. My twelve-year-old self-was irritated when the entertainment I'd looked forward to, was spoiled.

I reached over and turned off the radio, stomped out of the kitchen, and slammed the back door.

"Mama?" I queried, as I leaned over the metal railing on the back porch.

"I'm back here." Her voice came from behind the garage.

I scrambled down the cement steps to the driveway and walked along the path between the garage and the geranium-filled planter next to the patio.

When I rounded the corner of the garage, I spied her small frame, clad in a red-and-blue-plaid button-down-the-front housedress, topped by a faded red sweater, a hedge against the chilly winter air. Her short-cropped, wavy dark brown hair ruffled slightly in the breeze that always seemed to blow through the space along the side of our garage. A wicker clothes basket at her feet was nearly filled with neatly folded towels topped by an assortment of white underwear and colored socks.

"Mama," I said, anxiously. "I was listening to *The Great Gildersleeve* and it kept being interrupted. The announcer kept saying the Japanese have just bombed Pearl Harbor. Are they going to bomb us?"

"No," she replied in a calm voice. She continued to pluck clothespins from the crisp, dry garments and drop them in the basket. "They're a long way away. We don't have to worry." She paused. In a convincing tone, she added, "They aren't going to bomb us here."

I walked back into the house reassured by her words. But still disgruntled I hadn't been able to enjoy my favorite Sunday program.

Little did I know—or understand—but the world had changed that day—that historic Sunday, December 7, 1941

Monday morning began as usual. Mother fixed oatmeal with raisins and brown sugar and a sliced banana. She was adamant that we needed to begin the day with a nutritious breakfast.

We ate together as a family in the cheery kitchen. Daddy finished first, then left to walk down the hill to Colorado Boulevard and take the streetcar. He worked in downtown Los Angeles, in the Planning and Zoning Department in the City Hall.

Mother packed our lunch pails and sent my younger brother, and me off to school: Bunky with his pal, Bob Lawhan, (both in the fifth grade) for Dahlia Heights Elementary School, while I made my way down the street to my best friend Phyllis' house. We were both in the seventh grade and walked together to Eagle Rock Junior/Senior High School on Yosemite Blvd.

This was December 8th—the day after the Japanese had bombed Pearl Harbor.

We arrived at school shortly before nine o'clock, when our first-period class started. We sauntered towards the entrance and stood at the fringe of a group of girls clustered there. One of them, Lois, was telling the others, "My mom's *really* upset. Yesterday, when she heard the Japs had bombed

Hawaii she tried to reach my sister, who lives in Manilla. And she's been trying ever since."

Someone interrupted. "But it was Pearl Harbor that was bombed."

Tears glistened in Lois' brown eyes, "They also bombed Manilla."

I knew Pearl Harbor was in Hawaii but hadn't a clue about Manilla. In fact, I had only a vague idea where Japan was located.

In mid-morning, the principal, Miss Babson, called for an assembly. The combined junior and senior student body squeezed into the auditorium. She announced to the restive audience, "The United States has declared war on Japan." A hushed silence instantly descended over the gathering, like a sound-proof blanket. Not a foot shuffled. Not a whisper of clothing was heard. No one coughed. Nothing. No one moved. Then there was a collective gasp followed by scattered sounds of crying.

Hardly daring to move, I glanced furtively around and saw teachers dabbing their eyes as tears trickled down their cheeks. Others had their arms around some of the older girls holding them close while they sobbed. Even some of the older boys wrestled to maintain a "manly" stance and swiped vainly at escaping tears.

"Quiet. Please sit down. May I have your attention. Quiet," the principal implored, as she struggled to regain control. Finally, her pleas were heeded, and a modicum of silence returned to the now tense assembly.

She paused until quiet was restored, then continued. "To comply with safety regulations I received this morning, you can expect regular safety drills, and you may be directed to certain areas designated as bomb shelters. I'll be sending a note home with you today informing your parents of the measures the school will implement to ensure your safety."

Thank you for your attention. You are dismissed to go back to your classes. Please leave in an orderly manner."

We filed out, quiet and somber-faced—a contrast to the laughing, lively group who entered just a short time earlier.

Later, during the junior high lunch hour, Phillis and I were seated at a table outside, in the lunch quad. She looked over at me and asked, "Do you know *Patty Matthews? She's not in our class, she's still going to Dahlia Heights. But she lives near us, over on Dahlia Drive."

"No. I don't know her but I know who she is. What about her?"

"Well, she has two older brothers, one's a senior, and I think the other's a junior. Anyway, I heard her father's in the navy, and he was killed in the bombing yesterday in Pearl Harbor. Isn't that awful!"

I agreed. It was awful. But what does a twelve-year-old know about death? I did know it would terrible if it was my dad who had been killed.

This was just the first day of the United States' involvement in World War II. In the days that followed, there were many changes at school and school bus service was discontinued. All those affected had to take public transportation. There were no field trips. My friend Pat Bury, had to leave home very early in the morning to get to school since she came by bus and had to transfer several times.

The wood shop closed when the teacher was drafted. There was no one to replace him.

Air raid sirens became a familiar sound. We ducked under our desks and huddled there with our arms over our head until the all-clear sounded.

Inter-mural sporting events: basketball, baseball, football, and track were discontinued. All large gatherings were discouraged.

"Victory Rallies" were held weekly on the steps of the cafeteria that faced the lunch quad to encourage us to buy defense saving-stamps. The denominations of stamps were: 10- and 25-cents and were sold to help fund the war. A full booklet was worth $18.75, the price of a $25 war bond.

Some of the older girls married before their boyfriends went into the service and were sent overseas.

My Social Studies period always incorporated current events. We perused the newspaper for maps relating to battles in Europe and the Pacific and gained a knowledge of geography from them. An understanding of United States history was acquired by learning about its past wars. And I soon learned the location of Manilla—and Japan.

The teachers and staff were zealous in their efforts to provide as traditional a school experience as possible. They sponsored varied recreational activities: dances and sock-hops in the gym, athletic competitions between juniors and seniors on the football field, music and drama productions in the auditorium, and classic movies.

Only the fondest recollections spark my memory of those high school days. On the other hand, perhaps this is due to the mellowing effect of the passing decades. Certainly, they were "different" when compared with those of the previous and following generations. However, to those of us who were teenagers during those war years, they were *our* normal.

The mid-August sun made squiggly patterns on the flagstone patio as a barely perceptible afternoon breeze fluttered the leaves of the elm tree that shaded it. I was engaged in my favorite summertime "activity"—stretched out along the length of the comfy patio swing, a few library books beside me, one read and one to-be-read, and another open to the mystery I was engrossed in. A small bunch of icy cold green grapes on a napkin sat atop my belly. Mechanically, my fingers reached for a grape and plopped it in my mouth. I savored the refreshing juicy fruit and sighed with pleasure.

Suddenly, I stopped reading, fingers poised mid-air about to pluck another grape from the bunch. I sat up, surprised to hear Daddy's excited voice getting louder as he walked up the driveway.

"Carol? Bunky? Where are you?" he shouted.

"I'm out here," I called back. "On the patio. What's wrong? You're home early—it's only 4:30."

"Nothing's wrong," he answered as he bounded up the steps. "Nothing's wrong at all. In fact, everything's all right." I saw the huge smile that lit his face and his blue eyes twinkled with happiness.

"The war's ended! *That's* what's all right! Now, where's your Mother?"

My brother came up beside Daddy and asked, "Hi, Daddy. What's wrong?"

Daddy, usually on the reserved side, beamed as he repeated the news to my brother.

"Let's find your mother. We're going downtown to celebrate. Tootie," (Daddy's nickname for her) he called as he turned and went into the house. "Tootie. The war's over! The Japs surrendered. Let's drive downtown to watch the festivities."

After a quick dinner, we headed off. What should have been a half-hour drive took over an hour. We saw jubilant people gathered on street corners shouting and flashing the V for Victory sign at the passing cars. In response, they slowed, honked and flashed their headlights while the riders gestured back. Daddy grumbled under his breath about "all the traffic," and later as we neared the downtown, mumbled to no one in particular, "I'd better look for a place to park where we wouldn't be blocked in. I don't want to sit in a parking lot all night."

Dusk was falling as the distinctive, white tower of the 27-story city hall, where Daddy worked, came into view. It towered above the other buildings downtown, an icon of Los Angeles.

"Oh, my gosh," I said as I viewed it against the backdrop of the darkening sky. "Look at the city hall. The windows are all lit up, and there are outside lights are shining on it again. Doesn't it look beautiful? Wow!"

"Look! There are lights in *all* the buildings downtown!" Bunky said, in awe. "I almost forgot what the city looks like, all lit up like that."

"It's been a long time," Daddy said. "Almost four years. It looks like the blackout's over." We drove a few blocks in silence, dazzled by the sight of our hometown illuminated once more.

Spotting an empty space in a parking lot within walking distance of the inner city, Daddy hurriedly pulled in. As we exited the car, bedlam surrounded us. There were people everywhere. Happy people—laughing and shouting and waving. They rang bells and blew noisemakers. They linked arms and danced on the sidewalk and down the street.

"Stay together," Daddy hollered above the din. He took Mother's arm and hooked it into his own. "Carol, take my hand—Bunky, you hold on to Mother. We need to stay together. If we get separated, we'll *never* find one another in this crowd."

Off we went, south down Broadway. Exhilarated, we melded into the melee of slow-moving, exuberant humanity. The crowd grew as it moved toward the heart of downtown—like tiny trickles of water that merge to become the rushing torrent of a thunderous river. Except this was a virtual wave of revelers that filled the street. I felt like I was absorbing the sights and sounds, the sheer energy that surrounded us.

The sidewalks teemed with merrymakers. They walked shoulder-to-shoulder and overflowed into the street. There was barely enough room in the middle of the street to allow passage of horn-honking vehicles that inched forward. They overflowed with shouting passengers wildly waving small American flags out of the open windows or making the V-for-Victory sign with outstretched fingers. Some belted off-tune songs at the top of their lungs as they toasted America's victory with raised bottles of beer or whiskey. Euphoric hangers-on balanced precariously on the running boards, and clung, like leaches, from their perch on the front and back bumpers.

In the buildings that lined the street, people leaned from open windows, waving and shouting and throwing handfuls of confetti that wafted downward in the balmy summer air like misplaced snowflakes.

Windows in some of the stores must have been broken, as a deafening clang of activated burglar alarms added to the cacophony. A few policemen stood nearby but seemed disinclined to do anything about the triggered alarms. I guessed they were probably only there to protect the compromised property from vandalism.

Strangers hugged and kissed one another. Daddy, ever watchful, protected me, his almost sixteen-year-old daughter, from the overzealous and amorous clutches of one obviously intoxicated merrymaker. He good-naturedly remarked as he peeled the man's fingers from my arm, "Go find yourself a girl your own age, young man." The rebuffed man complied without a word and stumbled into the surging crowd to find a more willing subject for his euphoric advances.

As we were pushed and shoved along, we watched with fascination a conga-line of hundreds of chanting, swaying dancers. Like a giant reptile, it undulated as it zigzagged its way back and forth across the jammed street. It wove between the revelry-filled vehicles that moved at a snail's pace, jockeying for space amidst the crush of people.

Groups of servicemen seemed the most boisterous. They shouted the loudest and grabbed any willing body, male or female, within arm's reach to bestow a bear hug and a smooch. A cluster of sailors whooped and hollered and threw their caps in the air, seemingly oblivious of the plainly identified, but grinning, shore patrol and military police scattered throughout the crowd.

Block after block we shuffled along jostled and drawn forward by the riptide of the citizenry. The push and shove finally became too great. Daddy managed to herd us around a corner and down a side street for a few blocks.

"It's time we head back to the car," he bellowed above the pandemonium. Mother nodded in fervent agreement.

Like salmon headed upstream, we shouldered our way north on Main Street until we reached the parking lot. Fortunately, our car wasn't hemmed in, as some were, by an illegally parked vehicle. Daddy unlocked the doors and we dropped wearily onto our seats.

"Well!" Daddy said with a deep sigh as we sat for a moment in the idling car. "That was quite a celebration."

"It sure was," Mother said, her voice sounding tired. "But I wouldn't have missed it for anything."

Bunky and I merely nodded in agreement. We were too worn out by the festivities to reply.

The war in Europe had ended in June. But this was the country's final victory, the end of the war in the Pacific, and we had celebrated with all the energy and passion we could muster.   Looking back, it may also have been the zeal of a people ready to forge ahead into a world at peace—not one driven by war.

The year was 1945. During the intervening years, I've watched many events on TV, but nothing has generated the unequivocal emotion and joy that marked that occasion on August 14th.

Could it be because I was part of it?

Pirates of Jungle Gym Isle
By D. August Baertlein

MY BROTHER AND I GUARD our treasure from the pirates of Jungle Gym Isle. Today it's two gold medallions given to us by a serving wench in the kitchen.

"Take your cookies outside, boys," she says. "I don't want crumbs on the floor."

"But Mom," my brother says. "Those buccaneers out there will plunder our booty."

"Rival pirates, eh?" Mom looks thoughtful, then digs into her pantry. "Stow your cookies in this fine treasure chest." She hands us an old tin box with roosters painted on it.

"Roosters?" I say. "That ain't piratey!"

My brother shakes his head, "It's got no lock."

"Outside!" Mama points out the door to the realm of those thieving scallywags, the Pirates of Jungle Gym Isle. "Dad worked hard on that play structure," she says. "Now play, ye wee brigands. Play!"

I stash the gold medallions in that dumb rooster tin and tuck it under my vest. We unsheathe our swords, adjust our eye patches, and swagger out the door. Mom shuts it behind us. Haaaarrrrd.

Our boots have barely touched sand when my brother yells, "Pirates!" and sure enough, two scourges of the sea are sailing at us, fast.

Sally Longnose tries to distract us with her fancy zig-zag tacking, while Blackbeard takes a swipe at the treasure chest under my vest. I hold it close and show him the cold steel of my sword.

"ERRRR!" Blackbeard growls as he whooshes past, but I can see by his toothy smile he's just playing with me.

"To the ship!" I order (because I'm the captain today), and we scramble aboard our fine vessel, the *Lady Oak Tree*. "Ow!" A dangling acorn smacks my good eye. I switch my patch.

"I'll climb up to the crow's nest and keep watch on those brigands," my brother shouts.

"Aye! Good plan!" I say. "I'll stay behind and guard the treasure." But my belly growls and gives me away.

"Oh, no ye' don't, ye' scurvy rat." My brother snatches the treasure chest from my hand and starts to climb.

He makes it halfway up the rigging with our loot under his arm. Then a slip of his elbow sends it plummeting.

It bounces off the ship's mainmast.

"Arrgh!" he cries. It smacks the yardarm with a mighty whack.

"Curses!" I shout.

The treasure chest lands downside up under the hungry eyes of those pirate dogs. Painted roosters stare blindly up from the box, making no effort to defend our booty. I wish they could at least squawk a warning cry.

Blackbeard leaps on our treasure in a flash. But Sally pokes her long nose in and snags the box from under Blackbeard's stubby snout. She's off across the grassy sea, our booty clamped in her teeth, Blackbeard hot on her heels.

Round and round, they go, tail-flags flapping in the wind. Up and over Jungle Gym Isle they romp, then they splash through Blue Lagoon wading pool.

"After them!" my brother yells.

We leap from our ship, the *Lady Oak Tree*, draw our swords, and advance upon those thieving pirates.

"Avast, ye' mangy curs!" I shout. Sally slows to a trot.

"Sit!" I say in my deepest tough-pirate voice.

Sally stops. Her brown eyes roll to the left, then right. She sits back on her haunches. Blackbeard watches from the shadows.

I walk real slow right up to Sally Longnose. "Drop it," I say, "or it's the plank for ye'."

Sally drops the slobbery treasure into my hand, then stands at attention, tongue flopping out the side of her muzzle.

"Good lass." I scratch her behind the ears until she wags her big white flag of a tail.

"She surrenders!" my brother shouts, and we dance a pirate jig. Together we board the *Lady Oak Tree*, Sally Longnose, Blackbeard, my brother, and me. We sit in a circle on deck, just above the steep, steep plank that slides down to the grassy sea.

I open the treasure chest. My brother gasps.

"Our cookies!" he cries.

The two gold medallions are gone. In their place are a pile of gold dust and a scattering of golden nuggets.

Plenty to share.

My brother and I divvy up our treasure, leaving a few crumbs for the pirates of Jungle Gym Isle.

If you're going to have a story, have a big story, or none at all."
—Joseph Campbell

The Spirits of Whiskey Row
By Howard Gershkowitz

THE HISS AND RATTLE of the kitchen radiator couldn't cloak the fearsome bellows of the gale threatening to shatter the windows. The wind howled through the gables as I waited for the water to boil.

I stared at the stove's blue flames which whooshed sporadically, emitting a pungent smell as dust motes vaporized. The steam from the tea pot swirled, mingling with clouds emanating from my mouth and nose. Without warning, the burner winked out and an eerie silence replaced the chattering of the pipes.

Stepping into the hallway, I listened at the cellar door. The boiler should have been shouting and clanging as it produced its meager heat, but all I heard was the hopeless clicking of the firing nozzle. I opened the door and the gloom of the basement rose to meet me. A pull of the chord at the head of the stairs and the stingy illumination of a single bulb cast shadows on the floor below.

Climbing down the wooden escarpment, an icy dampness oozed from the walls, attacking my nostrils like the cold steel of bayonets. My good sense urged me to flee, to risk the storm outside rather than descend one step further.

I took a deep breath to calm my nerves. I regained my resolve and hurried past the boxes and dust-covered furniture scattered about to the furnace. I checked all the obvious concerns, but no ready solution presented itself—there was no dislocation of the nozzle nor an indication the oil supply was exhausted.

Something flashed behind me. The hair on the back of my neck stood instantly at attention. Turning slowly, I saw it. Seated squarely behind a roll-top desk was a man in top hat and formal attire. His face was ashen, his lips thin and colorless. Stringy, white strands of hair escaped his hat. His hook nose and wrinkled forehead betrayed old age. His eyes, however, were the most startling of his features, *for he had none*. No iris or pupil inhabited the hollow sockets. In their place, a reddish tinge of supernatural light escaped their empty confines.

Unable to move, I stared as the specter pointed a long, emaciated finger at me. Its mouth opened and from the depths of hell came a single word, *"DOOM!"*

Thousands of stinging, red ants crawled inside my skin. I breathed deeply, trying to stay conscious. Then the macabre image blinked out of existence, nothing left except a floating retinal image. I tried blinking it away to no avail. A thunderous cackle shattered the silence behind me and I whirled around, a scream at racing through my throat like a desert wind. I fully expected to see the ghoul on the attack. Instead, the boiler erupted back to life, the smell of sulfur heavy in the air. I turned tail and raced up the stairs, slamming the door behind me.

I leaned against it, my heart pounding in my ears, as the house returned to life. The pipes shook once more with their familiar clanging as hot water surged through them once again. Hidden subtly within the metallic chords of the old copper coils, however, was something different, something new; a sound I'd never heard previously.

It grew steadily louder, originating in the living room. I rushed into the kitchen towards the back door when the cacophony ceased abruptly. The unexpected silence caused me to look back. Another apparition appeared in the archway.

This poltergeist was ethereal and shifting, with no discernable features. I could see the stairs behind it through its silken folds as it hovered above the floor.

"Who are you? What do you want of me?" I asked, my voice trembling.

In response, it coalesced, churning and whirling like astral cotton candy. No longer transparent, images formed at its center, and I found myself staring at downtown Prescott, as if through a lens. The town's clock tower clearly displayed the time; 5:30. People were hurrying along Main Street.

As I watched, a fireball burst forth from the St. Michael's hotel obscuring the street with roiling orange and yellow flames. When the blast subsided, the hotel was engulfed in fire, the thick, black smoke rushing out splintered windows. Bodies lay on the ground and cars were ablaze up and down the street. The neighboring buildings caught fire as well. In the blink of an eye, the entire downtown was a roaring inferno.

The image faded, replaced by a new scene as if the ghoul had pressed fast forward on some celestial remote. Devastation was everywhere. Skeletons of vehicles threw off wisps of smoke. The clock tower, by some miracle, had survived, standing guard defiantly, frozen at 5:31.

The cosmic lens clouded over, and like the fog of melting dry ice, it floated to the ceiling, disappearing through the rafters.

I stood transfixed, blood pounding once more in my ears. The echoes of *doom* reverberated in my mind as I replayed the astral hologram over and over. Was it a curse? A premonition? And if so, what was I supposed to do about it? I could spread the alarm, but who'd believe me? Mayor Jessup was unlikely to evacuate the town on my say-so, not without proof.

I looked at the digital clock on the wall, the bright red numerals reminiscent of the first specter. It was past midnight, but I couldn't sleep now. The spirits had chosen to retire, at least temporarily, and I needed a plan.

***

"A bomb, you say? At the St. Michael's?" Tom Jessup said, eyeing me with skepticism. Mayor for the last six years, his family had been early settlers, operating the Bar J ranch on the Southern edge of the Yavapai River since the1890's.

"I said maybe. I don't know for sure. It could be the gas lines are rigged to rupture," I said, sticking to my hastily contrived script.

"And tell me again how you know this?"

"Like I said, I stopped for coffee at the cafe and overheard two men talking. They were behind the partition between the restaurant and lobby. *'It oughta blow at 5:30. It'll be a heck of a sight, I figger,'* one of them whispered. The other one said, *'we'd best be long gone. I don't want to end up no crispy critter.'*"

"So, you figured they meant the hotel was going to blow up tonight at 5:30?"

"Wouldn't you?"

"Why didn't you tell Jake? I'm sure he would have investigated immediately."

"I *did* tell him! He didn't believe me—thought I was telling tales."

"Are you? Cause if I order an evacuation and nothing happens, you're going to be in big trouble, Bill."

"I'm not telling tales and I'm not telling you what to do. I heard what I heard. If something happens and people die, it'll be on your head, not mine."

He scratched the stubble on his chin.

"It's only 10:30. I'll call Sam down at the Sherriff's, have him meet us at the hotel. No use alarming the guests just yet. We'll evacuate if we find anything suspicious."

"And what if we don't find anything right off? What then?"

"Then it'll just be your imagination gone wild, understand? I don't want a panic, and I expect you to keep this between us till I say otherwise, understand?"

"Understood," I said.

***

The St. Michael was built soon after the fire on Whiskey Row in 1900 which destroyed a good portion of the town. The furnace and feeder lines for all the modern, gas-fed fireplaces ran in a grid below the main floor, located behind a solid oak door leading to the basement, a sturdy behemoth with a modern steel lock intended to last another hundred years.

Tom, Sam and I methodically traced the pipes and wires lining the beams above us. We picked through the graveyard of long-forgotten furnishings and spittoons. It felt like the catacombs of France, though less musty and without the requisite piles of decaying bones.

"What exactly should we be looking for?" I asked.

"Anything out of place," Sheriff Sam Goldstein said. "Keep your eyes open for recently disturbed furniture or signs of fresh sawdust. Tom and I will check out the boiler."

"What about the gas company?" I asked.

"Already called them. A repair team is on standby just in case."

"You know," Tom said, "the town was nearly destroyed a couple of times by fire. The first one in 1900 was caused by a careless miner who left his mining candle burning near a wall in one of the saloons. You think some laid-off, disgruntled miner is trying to repeat it on purpose?"

Sam didn't answer directly but turned to me instead. "You have any idea who those two fellas were you overheard, Bill?"

"They didn't sound familiar."

"And you didn't think to peek around the partition to get a look?"

"I did, but they were gone before I could."

"And you don't remember anything else that might be useful?"

"If I did, I'd tell you, wouldn't I?"

"Keep thinking—maybe something will come back to you." He and Tom headed off to check out the boiler.

'There were these two ghosts, you see…'

Two hours later, having found nothing suspicious, Tom called the search off.

"Looks like you sent us on a wild goose chase, Bill," Sam said as we stood outside of the hotel.

"I'm telling you, I heard what I heard. Something bad's gonna happen here tonight. I feel it in my bones."

"Well, I can't order an evacuation because you've got arthritis," Tom said. "Just be glad I don't have Sam arrest you for wasting our time. Next time you hear voices, go see an ear doctor. I have a council meeting to prep for." With that, he turned and stomped away.

The clock tower chimed 1 pm.

Back in the hotel, I found the bellhop who'd unlocked the door to the lower sanctum. "Sorry to bother you again," I said, "seems I left my cell phone downstairs."

He nodded and unlocked the basement door again.

"Thanks. I'll find my own way out."

In the main furnace room, I repeated my search for obvious problems, as I did in my own basement the previous evening. There were no observable misalignments or frayed wires and no tell-tale odor of rotten eggs to indicate a gas leak.

Next, I meticulously retraced the gas lines crisscrossing the basement paying careful attention at each junction disappearing through the floor above me.

Glancing at my watch, I realized two more hours had passed. I removed a dusty sheet from an old wicker chair and sat down to gather my thoughts. Stretching my neck, I noticed a wisp of smoke around the pipe just above me. It didn't dissipate however. It casually floated there, suspended in space. Then a second wisp appeared, and then another, like strands of cotton candy forming around the copper. The tingling at the back of my neck returned. The strands condensed into a long, thin rope, wrapping itself around the pipe. It moved along its length like a snake. I followed, staying a good twenty feet back. Finally, it stopped and formed a small, white ball around an elbow joint I'd surveyed ten minutes ago. The ball brightened sharply, then exploded like a sun going nova. Then it blinked out entirely leaving me momentarily blinded. When my eyes readjusted, the smoke creature was gone, but in its place, I saw a bulge in the joint just below the floorboards.

4:15 pm.

I jumped the stairs two at a time, nearly smashing my face when the knob turned but the door didn't open. It took a second to realize it was locked. I shouted for help, pounding on the wood.

4:18 pm.

Then it hit me—it was check n time! Everyone was at the front of the hotel with the arriving guests. Racing down the stairs I searched for another exit. Breathing deep to control the panic, I found no unexpected doors or boarded windows. I scoured the floorboards above me for a trap door or hidden, collapsible stairs.

In desperation, I started overturning the furniture and boxes along the walls. I worked furiously but stopped when a flash erupted behind me. Turning, I spotted an old desk on the south wall. A figure sat there, this time with its back to me. I could make out the top hat and scraggly, white hair. It didn't turn to face me this time. I watched as two beams of red light shot from its hidden eyes, forming a slender laser beam. It glinted off something on the wall, splitting into a crimson spider web.

Then it vanished again.

I walked towards the desk, finding death by haunting preferable to death by fire. It was empty, but on the wall where the beams converged was a rusted nut and bolt. Pushing the desk aside, I found several more holding a rusted steel plate in place. *Of course!* There were no gas lines here in 1901, but there was plenty of coal.

Scouring the immediate area for something to pry the plate from the wall, I tripped on a wooden box. Opening it I found several shovels and a pickaxe, rusted but functional. Grabbing it, I struck the flat blade against the first bolt, snapping it like a dry twig. Three more swings and the remaining nuts broke off.

Stepping back, I swung the pointed end of the ax at the top of the place. There was a loud, metal clang and a small separation appeared. Placing the flat end into the opening now, I leaned heavily on the handle. It moved slowly at first, but then gave way with an ear-splitting shriek.

Sunlight framed the ax handle in my hands. I looked up the exposed shaft; a wooden hatch covered it, some eight feet above me, the dusty rays streaming through the weathered boards.

The sides of the chute were too slippery to climb so I reached up with the ax and hooked it between two of the planks. I pulled myself up, wedging against the sides by pushing with my legs to keep my back secure against the opposite wall. I broke apart the boards, one by one before dropping the ax and pulling my body through the opening.

I was in the alley behind the hotel. Racing around the corner, I emerged on the street and came face to face with the town's clock tower.

5:10 pm: There wasn't time to find Tom or Sam. The gas company's office was up on Sheldon Street, two blocks away so I sprinted up the sidewalk. I was winded in less a block and a half, so I half walked, half jogged till I reached the front door and pushed on it.

When it didn't open, I cursed. *Damned banker's hours.* It was after 5 pm and they were closed for the day. Peering in a side window, I spotted an employee sitting at a desk. He looked up when I rapped on the glass but just shook his head and pointed at this watch. I stepped back towards the street and found a suitable rock. The window shattered with a loud bang as the glass shards erupted from the casement. The man appeared at the window, shouting, but I shouted louder and with more enthusiasm;

"There's no time to spare. There's a gas leak at the St Michael's, and it's likely to blow any second. You have to shut off the gas any way you can. There are hundreds of people in that hotel, and they'll all be dead if you don't act *right now!*"

"What?" he said, and then it sank in. He rushed back to his desk and picked up the telephone. By his arm gesticulations, I could tell he was belching orders to someone on the other end of the line.

Exhausted, I turned back towards the street. I was about to check my watch when I heard a loud bang and cried out, collapsing to the ground. *Too late.*

Something touched my shoulder and I nearly jumped out of my skin. I jerked my head around to see a young boy staring down at me. "Don't be scared, mister. My Dad's car always backfires like that. He says it has to do with the carb'rator or somethin'."

I stared at him in disbelief. Getting up, I rushed back to Gurley Street. The hotel was unharmed; no fire or smoke spewing from its windows. Several utility vehicles were pulling up along with a police cruiser.

The hands on the clock tower announced it was 5:32pm.

Seated at the massive, formal dining table at the Bar J Ranch, I exchanged pleasantries with Sam and his lovely wife, Diane.

"Your quick thinking saved a lot of lives, Bill," Tom said as he joined us at the table. "But one thing still bothers me. That crazy story of yours about a bomb…"

"I told you— they never said 'bomb.' I stuck to my story."

"Okay, so how'd they arrange for the gas line rupture? The fire marshal's report cited metal fatigue. Pure circumstance, and pure luck you found it."

"How should I know? I mean, after all…"

"But you said '5:30'. You were very specific. What aren't you telling me?"

"Nothing. I'm telling you the tru…."

My eyes caught a picture on the wall behind Bill. He caught my stare and turned to look.

"Oh, that old picture? That's my great granduncle, Eldon and his wife, Clarice. I found it in the attic recently and decided to put it up."

Eldon looked serious and dapper sitting at an accountant's desk, dressed formally in a tuxedo and top hat with gray hairs protruding. His eyes, focused on the camera, appeared reddened from the flash. Clarice stood beside him, elegant and ethereal in her flowing, white gown with lace accents.

"They look like a happy couple," I muttered.

"So, I've been told," Tom said. "I never met them. They died in 1900, during the great fire."

***

Great is the art of beginning but greater is the art of ending.
—Henry Wadsworth Longfellow

17178421R00093

Made in the USA
San Bernardino, CA
22 December 2018